TAKE JENNINGS,
FOR INSTANCE

More Jennings books to watch out for:

Author's note

Each of the Jennings books is a story complete in itself. Apart from the first title, JENNINGS GOES TO SCHOOL, the books can be read in any order, and for this reason I have chosen some of the later titles for early publication in this edition.

Anthony Buckeridge

TAKE JENNINGS, FOR INSTANCE

Anthony Buckeridge

**MACMILLAN
CHILDREN'S BOOKS**

To the 'Jennings Club'
of Warden House School

First published 1958 by
William Collins & Sons Co Ltd

Paperback edition published 1994 by
MACMILLAN CHILDREN'S BOOKS
A division of Macmillan Publishers Limited
London and Basingstoke
Associated companies throughout the world

ISBN 0–333–61133–0

3 5 7 9 8 6 4 2

A CIP catalogue record for this book is available from
the British Library

Phototypeset by Intype, London
Printed by Cox & Wyman Ltd, Reading

CONTENTS

List of Illustrations

Chapter 1

The Naturalists

Jennings gazed at the tadpoles in solemn wonder, unable to take his eyes away from the plump, pear-shaped globules wriggling to and fro in the pond water at the bottom of the jamjar. They seemed to be in such a hurry – darting about in spirals and zigzags like crotchets and quavers trying to escape from a sheet of music . . .

Busy folk, these pond dwellers! Keen tadpoles, working their way up to become successful frogs, could not afford to take life easily, it seemed! And that raised another point, Jennings reflected as he eased the jamjar into his blazer pocket: did they *know* they were going to turn into frogs? Could they count on it, in the same way that he and Darbishire knew that one day they would be grown up with deep voices and long trousers – and, perhaps, even large curly moustaches? . . . It was difficult to decide. He would get Darbishire to make a note of this debatable point in his Nature Diary. Later on would be time enough for that, though, when they could study the habits of these budding amphibians at their leisure. At the moment, the thing to do was to collect as many specimens as they could find.

With a steadying hand on the makeshift aquarium in his pocket, Jennings turned and squelched his way to the far side of the pond, where his fellow naturalist, kneeling in the mud, was scribbling on a scrap of paper supported on the sole of an old boot which he had salvaged from the water.

"Hey, Darbi, I've just caught another batch of tadpoles. Bung them down on the inventory," Jennings called out as he approached.

Darbishire broke off from his clerical labours and blinked at his friend through mud-splashed spectacles.

"Give me a chance, Jen. I haven't finished recording the first lot yet."

"Well, get a move on. We'll have them hatching out into frogs before they've been registered as tadpoles at this rate. Just put: *16.23 hours. Six decent-sized specimens rounded up by J. C. T. Jennings, Chief Spotter, Frog and Tadpole Department*."

"I can't put all that on this titchy little bit of paper," Darbishire complained. "It'll have to wait till I go indoors and copy it out properly."

The eleven-year-old secretary of the Form Three Natural History Club took his duties seriously. This was only to be expected, for Charles Edwin Jeremy Darbishire was of an earnest disposition. He had a distinctive voice and a deliberate way of stressing certain words which somehow gave the impression that he was speaking in capital letters. Solemn in appearance and cautious by nature, he was a loyal follower with no ambitions to become a leader.

In this he differed from his friend, Jennings, a lively, impulsive boy of the same age, with a wide-awake look in his eyes and a ready enthusiasm to take command in most of the activities of school life.

"Seen anything else worth putting in the record?" Jennings asked as he squeezed the muddy water from a white cotton sock which he had been using as a fishing net.

"I saw a moorhen," Darbishire replied. "As a matter of fact, I've been making up a poem about it. You see, I thought it'd be a good idea to do a drawing of a bird on the cover of the Nature Diary, and then put some home-made poetry underneath – illustrated by the author, if you see what I mean."

Jennings was not impressed. "It's not supposed to be that sort of book at all. It's got to be a strictly scientific record of wildlife, not a lot of weedy poetry!"

"It won't be weedy! You wait till you hear it. I think I shall call it *The Feathered Songster*."

"You'll call it *what*?"

"It means bird, really," Darbishire explained in his capital-letter voice. "After all, we've got bird-watching down on our list of things to do, as well as frog-spotting, don't forget. Would you like to hear it?"

"No, not much."

"Well, I'll tell you, then," the poet went on unabashed. "It starts off:

Hark how the feathered songster sings,
As it flies on rumpty-tumpty wings."

3

"Funny sort of poem," said Jennings. "Funny sort of wings, too."

"Well, actually I got a bit stuck on the second line. It isn't finished yet, but it'll come out all right in the end."

"I dare say. But I can't stay here all afternoon listening to rumpty-tumpty poetry recitals," Jennings said firmly. "I'm going back to the other side of the pond to see if I can find any newts."

One of the chief attractions of the pond at Linbury Court was that it was situated at the farthest end of the grounds, well away from the main school buildings grouped round the quadrangle, and beyond the cricket and football pitches which stretched from the head-master's garden to the overgrown wilderness of shrubs and bushes where the land was low-lying and marshy. Here, on the edge of the pond, the keen naturalist could hunt for tadpoles after cricket on a fine half-holiday, secure in the knowledge that his movements would not be visible to the master on duty supervising the knock-about games of French cricket and rounders taking place on the playing-field.

During the Christmas and Easter terms, the wood and the pond were out of bounds, but with the return of summer weather the ban was relaxed so that the natural-ists could pursue their hobby.

Mr Pemberton-Oakes, the headmaster, made this con-cession with mixed feelings. In theory, the Form Three Natural History Club was an undertaking worthy of encouragement and support – an admirable pastime for a summer afternoon. In practice, however, he found that the study of wildlife upset the smooth running of school rou-tine in the most distressing fashion. Torn clothing, scratched knees, sodden footwear, caterpillars escaping in the classroom, beetles at large in the basement, spiders' eggs hatching out on the radiators, dead leaves, puddles of pond water. And everywhere a clutter of cardboard boxes teeming with insect life – these were the inevitable results of the boys' zeal for zoology.

The headmaster did his best to be fair and to take a reasonable view. The Natural History Club was permitted to flourish, but over its head hung the threat that it would be banned at a moment's notice if its activities showed signs of getting out of hand.

This warning was present in Darbishire's mind as he watched his friend preparing to extend his search to the other side of the pond.

"Be careful! It's terribly soggy round those parts, Jen," he said. "I got plastered with mud last time I went over there, and wet right through to my socks. Matron didn't half create."

"What of it? I'm not afraid of a bootful of water."

"No, but . . ." The secretary narrowed his brows in a frown of caution. "Well, don't make a row, that's all. We don't want everyone to know we're down by the pond."

"Don't be so fussy, Darbi. We're allowed to come here."

"Yes, I know, but Mr Wilkins said the other day that the Archbeako would put it out of bounds again if many more people got their feet wet."

Jennings snorted. "Huh! Just like grown-ups! They say, 'Why don't you start a Natural History Club?' and as soon as you *do* start one they kick up a hoo-hah and threaten to stop it in case you get your shoes muddy. Anyway, I'm going to look for some newts, whatever anyone says."

5

"Righto, then." Darbishire rose to his feet, his knees squelching out of the mud with a faint plopping sound. "D'you want me to come with you?"

"No, you stay here. I'm going alone ... All on my rumpty-tumpty own." A broad grin spread over Jennings' face. "How's that for home-made poetry, Darbi? And without thinking, too." He turned and splashed his way along the edge of the pond, pausing every few steps to make sure that none of the tadpoles had escaped from the jamjar in his pocket.

As he reached the farther end, where the rushes grew in tall, thick clumps, he heard, away to his left, the crackling of twigs breaking underfoot. Someone was approaching through the little wood that lay between the pond and the playing-field. Perhaps it was Venables, or Atkinson, or some other Club member coming to report his observations to the secretary.

Jennings peered through a gap in the bulrushes, mildly curious to know which of his colleagues was returning. Suddenly he stopped still, a hail of greeting frozen to silence on his lips. For it was not Venables, or Atkinson, or, indeed, any other youthful naturalist. It was Mr Carter, the senior master.

The next second a deep voice rang out. "Who is that boy over there? ... Is there anyone in those reeds?"

For a moment Jennings hesitated. He was breaking no rule in being behind the pond, and yet in his muddy, dishevelled state he had no wish to present himself for the master's inspection if it could be avoided. After all, it was against an encounter of this sort that Darbishire had just issued a warning. Perhaps, if he remained quiet, Mr Carter could be persuaded into thinking that no one was there after all, or even that the rustling sounds were caused by some water fowl making its way through the bulrushes.

Jennings was rather proud of his ability to imitate the call of a moorhen. If Mr Carter should call again . . .

At that moment Mr Carter *did* call again. "Is there anyone in those reeds? Answer me at once, do you hear?"

Without hesitation, the answer came back loud and clear. "*Quark, quark, quark!*" croaked Jennings, in what he hoped was a lifelike impression of a moorhen calling to its young.

"Oh, so it's you, is it, Jennings. I'd know that voice anywhere," Mr Carter said promptly. "Come here – I want to speak to you."

The bogus moorhen sighed in despair. It was impossible to fool Mr Carter. However hard you tried, the man refused to be baffled, and always saw through any plan devised to put him off the scent.

In spite of this blemish in his character, the senior assistant master was liked and respected by all the boys at Linbury Court. He was a quietly spoken man of middle age who had been a schoolmaster long enough to have learnt a great deal about what went on in the minds of the boys whom he taught. He could, therefore, be relied upon to listen to their troubles with a friendly ear and to dispense justice with understanding.

"That was *not* a very good imitation of a moorhen, Jennings," he remarked as the boy emerged from the reeds.

"No, sir."

"It sounded more like a cement mixer grinding a shovelful of gravel."

"Sorry, sir."

7

"What were you doing over there?"

It was difficult to provide a short answer to this question, for an excursion to the far side of the pond always gave rise to a variety of interesting occupations.

"Do you mean just now, sir?" Jennings asked, playing for time.

"Of course I mean just now. You don't imagine I mean the term before last, do you? What were you doing in the reeds when I called to you?"

"Just coming out, sir."

Mr Carter clicked his tongue in patient rebuke.

"And before that?"

"I was frog-spotting, sir. It's like bird-watching, only different."

"H'm. It obviously doesn't require the same degree of stealth and cautious movement," the master observed. "I could see the reeds waving about like semaphore flags from the other side of the cricket square."

"That was Darbishire, sir. He thought he saw a water-rat, but it was only an old boot," Jennings explained. "You see, he's secretary of our Natural History Club, and I'm Chief Spotter of the Frog and Tadpole Department."

As he spoke, the reeds parted again and the secretary came out into the open clutching his precious scrap of paper.

"Yes, that's right, sir," Darbishire affirmed, as he climbed the bank. "I have to write everything down, like, say, for instance, wild creatures and plants and stuff observed by the pond, and ... and anything seen flying about overhead, too, sir."

"And what have you observed in flight this afternoon?"

Darbishire frowned in thought. "Two starlings and a jet

8

aircraft, sir," he reported. "Of course, the aircraft doesn't really count, even though it was . . ."

The explanation tailed off as he became aware that the master was eyeing their unkempt appearance with disfavour. The sodden shoes and socks, the mud-caked knees, the damp patches on trousers and blazers told their own story.

Finally Mr Carter said, "Listen to me, you two. I am all in favour of your Natural History Club. In fact, I'm thinking of asking the headmaster to let you go farther afield to collect more specimens outside the school grounds . . ."

"Thank you, sir. Really great of you, sir."

". . . but there won't be much chance of that happening if the Club is banned in the mean time because of the state you are in," Mr Carter went on. "You know the rule about not getting your clothes dirty. Just look at your shoes and socks!"

"It'll brush off, sir," said Jennings, wiping his muddy blazer with hands which were even muddier.

"That's not the point. I'm warning you that you are liable to have all these interesting pond-side activities stopped if you don't watch your step."

"Yes, sir."

"And take that jamjar out of your pocket. It's ruining the shape of your blazer."

Gingerly Jennings removed the temporary aquarium and then shot an anxious glance at Mr Carter. "But we can keep these tadpoles now that we've caught them, can't we, sir?"

The master nodded. "Yes, all right. And now go indoors and tidy yourselves up. Mr Wilkins won't want you going in to tea looking like a couple of scarecrows."

So saying, he turned and retraced his steps towards the playing-field where his ever-roving eye had just caught sight of Binns and Blotwell, the youngest boys in the school, doing a war dance on the forbidden territory of the First XI cricket pitch.

As they dawdled their way back to the school buildings, Jennings and Darbishire were joined by a small group of fellow naturalists returning from a similar expedition in search of specimens. Venables, a tall, thin boy of eleven, with untidy hair and trailing shoe-laces, was deep in conversation with his friend, Temple, a stocky, square-rigged youth of about the same age. Beside them trotted Atkinson, carrying a cigar box with holes bored through the lid.

"Hallo, you lot!" Jennings greeted them. "Been doing any famous exploits for the Club?"

Venables shrugged. "We tried to, but it was a wash-out. We started off looking for puss-moths' eggs, only we couldn't find any so we built a bird-watching shelter, instead."

"Great idea," Darbishire approved.

"Huh! We'd only just got started when the Archbeako came stonking up and ticked me off for tearing my sweater!"

Jennings nodded in sympathy. "Mouldy chizz! We just can't do a thing without someone butting in these days. We went frog-spotting, only Mr Carter started moaning because we'd got a titchy little splash of pond water on our shoes. Still, we got some more tadpoles for ye aquarium," he finished up, thrusting the jamjar under Venables' nose.

By this time the little group had reached the concrete path leading to the rear entrance of the school. On one side was a row of outbuildings comprising the carpenter's shop, the bicycle shed and two garages where assistant masters kept their cars.

The doors of one garage were open, and the rear end of Mr Wilkins' dark red saloon car was visible inside. One glance at the old-fashioned bodywork revealed that the vehicle was no recent model, but in spite of its age and rather battered appearance its owner was proud of the car's sterling performance and spent a fair amount of time in keeping it in a roadworthy condition.

To the boys of Linbury Court School, Mr Wilkins' car was something of a joke. The sight of it parked on the playground or chugging unsteadily down the drive would often call forth some unflattering remark – provided, of course, that the proud owner was safely out of earshot.

As usual, it was Jennings who drew attention to the shortcomings of the vintage model.

"Look at Sir's ancient old cronk! It reminds me of something that's escaped from the Science Museum," he observed as they drew level with the garage. "I bet it couldn't do a mile in four minutes, not even downhill with the wind behind it!"

Darbishire tittered in appreciation. "It might, if you gave it a good shove to start it off," he suggested.

"If you gave it a shove, you'd push it right off its rockers," Jennings replied derisively. "Mind you, it would be all right as a mobile rabbit-hutch, but as for . . ."

"*Jennings!*"

The interruption came so unexpectedly that Jennings broke off in sudden alarm, his hand flying to his mouth in guilty dismay . . . For the deep, booming voice belonged to Mr Wilkins, and it appeared to be coming from below

11

ground level, like some angry volcano giving warning of explosions to follow.

The mystery of the ventriloquial voice was solved a moment later when Mr Wilkins' face appeared beneath the back number plate of the car. The face was followed by a pair of broad shoulders as the master eased himself out from beneath the chassis where he had been inspecting the oil level in the rear axle.

Jennings went pink with embarrassment, and the rest of the group shuffled uncomfortably from foot to foot. True, it was not a punishable offence to express an opinion about someone else's property. All the same, tactless comments of this kind did little to improve friendly relations and establish a happy atmosphere between masters and boys.

Mr Wilkins rose to his full height. He was a tall, energetic man with a loud, booming voice and a heavy footstep. An impatient nature and a brusque manner concealed the fact that he was fond of the boys committed to his care. Unfortunately he lacked the insight and understanding of his colleague Mr Carter, and was thus unable to appreciate the reasons behind some of the more peculiar antics of the rising generation.

"Come here, Jennings, you horrible little boy!" Mr Wilkins said. "If I hear any more funny remarks from you about my car I shall – I shall . . . Well, there'd better not *be* any more funny remarks!"

"Yes, sir. I mean, no, sir. I didn't mean to – that is, I'm terribly sorry, sir," Jennings stammered.

"So you should be." Mr Wilkins' tone was gruff, though in point of fact he was not at all perturbed by the facetious remarks. Owners of old cars soon grew used to comments of that kind. Still, it was bad for discipline to let imperti-

nence go unchecked, he reflected, and anyway, it would do
the boy no harm to be taken down a peg or two.

Loudly he barked, "Disgraceful behaviour! You'd
better watch your step, Jennings, or you'll find yourself in
serious trouble before the term's much older."

In this Mr Wilkins was right, though it could hardly be
classed as a brilliant prophecy, for Jennings was seldom
out of trouble for very long.

The master frowned at the group, noting their muddy
appearance, and then his glance came to rest upon the
half-filled jamjar.

"What's that revolting collection of squirming specimens you've got in there?" he demanded.

"Only a few tadpoles, sir," replied Jennings. "Mr Carter
said we could."

"Yes, that's right, he did," Darbishire confirmed. "Sir
gave us permish to keep them, sir."

Mr Wilkins winced and drew in his breath sharply,
"*Who* gave you *what*, Darbishire?"

"Sorry, sir. I mean, Mr Carter gave us permission, sir."

"So I should think. *Sir gave you permish!*" Mr Wilkins
tut-tutted like thimbles on a washing-board. "Why can't
you boys learn to express yourselves in English! Where
are you going to keep the things, anyway?"

"On the common-room window-sill, sir," Jennings
answered. "Bromwich has got an old goldfish tank you
see, sir, and . . ."

"Tadpoles in the common-room! Not if I know it!"

"Oh, but, sir! Mr Carter said we could! It's all part of
the Form Three Natural History Club, sir," the secretary
explained. "We got them specially so we can observe wildlife and stuff."

"Please can't we keep them, sir? They won't get out or

run away or anything," Venables pleaded. "Just a few quiet tadpoles that wouldn't hurt a fly, sir."

"H'm. Well, if Mr Carter says so, I suppose it's all right," Mr Wilkins conceded grudgingly. "But I'm warning you boys, if they become a nuisance I shall – I shall . . ." Once more he searched his mind for a fitting punishment. Somewhat lamely he finished up, "Well, they'd better *not* become a nuisance, that's all!"

In chastened mood the little group moved on in silence, while Mr Wilkins frowned after them until they turned the corner. Then he switched off his forbidding expression and hummed gently to himself as he crawled back underneath the car to resume his labours.

Chapter 2

Future Plans

"Phew! I thought you'd had it that time, Jen," Venables observed as he led the way into the common-room a few minutes later. "You want to be careful what you say about Old Wilkie's clanking old gridiron. He's got supersonic ear-sight."

"Well, how was I to know he was hiding underneath," Jennings defended himself. "Anyway, he didn't stop us bringing the tadpoles in, and that's the main thing."

He hurried across to the window-sill where Bromwich's goldfish tank had been adapted to serve as an aquarium for assorted pond-dwellers. Here, tadpoles and water-beetles, caught on previous expeditions, were skimming about on their ceaseless journeys. Flanking the aquarium on either side and stretching all along the window-sill were cardboard boxes with perforated lids housing insects of every description.

Carefully, Jennings tipped the most recent additions

into the tank to join their wriggling colleagues, and then turned to assist Temple in rounding up an escaping caterpillar which had already scaled the common-room wall and was scurrying along the picture rail in a bid for freedom.

Darbishire, meanwhile, had taken the Nature Diary from his locker and sat down at a table to enter the results of the afternoon's work. He had begun keeping this record at the beginning of the term and he was proud of the fact that the notebook provided a detailed account of the Club's activities. On the first page was a list of members with a brief description of the duties assigned to each.

"PRIVATE AND CONFIDENTIAL," announced Page One in wobbling capitals. "The following persons are hereby allowed to belong to the Club but not anybody else:

Venables, G. J.	*Chief Bird Watcher*
Temple, C. A.	*Curator of Caterpillars*
Bromwich, D.	*Head Newt Keeper*
Atkinson, R.	*Moles and Voles (if any)*
Jennings, J. C. T.	*Chief Spotter, Frog and Tadpole Department*
Darbishire, C. E. J.	*Hon Sec*
Martin-Jones, A. L.	*Beetles and small stuff*
Rumbelow, D. W.	*Odd jobs and Fodder."*

The list occupied a whole page and was followed by observations, progress reports and a complicated attendance register showing the total amount of wildlife in stock.

In his best handwriting Darbishire made a note of the tadpoles Jennings had caught during the afternoon. Then,

16

on a page headed "Future Plans," he wrote: "June 6th. Mr C. said he would get permish for us to go and look for things outside school grounds."

He was blotting this entry with his handkerchief when he remembered that they had not yet obeyed Mr Carter's orders.

"Hey, Jennings, hadn't we better go and give our knees and things a bit of a rinse?" he queried. "The tea bell will be going in a minute, and Old Wilkie's on duty, don't forget."

Jennings replaced the straying caterpillar in its box and said, "He won't see our knees if they're underneath the table."

"No, but . . ." Darbishire did not believe in taking unnecessary risks. "Well, you know what Mr Carter said – about seeing the Archbeako and all that."

"Maybe you're right," Jennings conceded, turning towards the door. "Come on, then, let's go and spruce up a bit. Sir seems to be on our side at the moment, so we'd better not give him an excuse to change his mind."

Mr Carter was as good as his word. A few days later he broached the subject to the headmaster in the staff-room during mid-morning break.

"By the way, HM, I'd like a word with you about the Form Three Natural History Club," he began.

A shadow of doubt flickered in the headmaster's eyes. "Yes, of course, Carter. I quite agree that it's high time we took steps to curb their – ah – their depredations. Matron tells me that she found a swarm of newly hatched water-beetles swimming about in a wash-basin in Dormitory Four. Obviously they'd been put there by . . ."

"Quite," Mr Carter interposed hastily. "But what I had in mind was . . ."

". . . and that wasn't all," Mr Pemberton-Oakes went on, heedless of the interruption. "Take Jennings, for instance: only the other day I had to reprimand him for – for . . ." The headmaster wrinkled his brows in thought. There were so many things for which he had had to reprimand Jennings that he couldn't remember the details of the case in point. "Well, I know it was something to do with insects," he said vaguely.

"Exactly. The boys are so keen on collecting specimens and making first-hand observations that I feel we should give them every encouragement," Mr Carter maintained.

"I dare say, Carter. And in theory I quite agree that their interest in Natural History is most – ah – most praise-worthy. It is instructive; it is educational. I don't deny that. But at the same time we cannot allow these happy-hunting third-formers to turn the entire school premises into a caterpillar sanctuary. If we allow this sort of thing to continue unchecked . . ." The headmaster broke off as the circumstances of his encounter with Jennings came back into his mind. "Ah, yes, I remember now. Take Jennings, for instance! . . . Believe it or not, Carter, I found him out of bounds in the kitchen garden examining the potato plants in the hope of finding a Colorado beetle." Mr Pemberton-Oakes shook his head in disapproval. He looked upon himself as a tolerant and kindly man. But really! This flagrant trespassing was carrying things too far.

"That's very interesting," said Mr Carter, undismayed by what the headmaster seemed to regard as a horrifying revelation. "It rather suggests that the boys need a chance to carry on the good work where they can't do any damage. That's what I wanted to see you about, as a matter of fact. I'd like to take them on a natural history excursion one Saturday, when we haven't got a match."

The headmaster pursed his lips and fingered his chin thoughtfully. Perhaps Carter was right. If the boys were allowed to work off their surplus zeal in some uncultivated strip of open country, the plants in the school garden would have a better chance of survival.

"Very well then, Carter. I see no objection," he decided. "What sort of excursion had you in mind?"

"The best plan would be to take a party on bicycles to the river valley just this side of Dunhambury," Mr Carter replied promptly. He had worked out all the arrangements in detail before making the proposal. "If you'd allow them to miss the last lesson in the morning, we could get there before lunch time and have a picnic. That would give them the whole afternoon for studying the wildlife of the district."

"Splendid!" Mr Pemberton-Oakes approved.

"Perhaps you'd like to come too, HM?"

"Naturally, I should be delighted to – ah – to . . ." The headmaster paused for reflection. On the last school picnic he had attended, he had unwittingly sat on an anthill and had been plagued by wasps buzzing round his sandwiches at every bite. "On second thoughts, though, Carter, I doubt whether I can spare the time. Pressure of work, you know; pressure of work."

Mr Carter had organised picnics on many previous occasions, but his plans for this latest excursion differed from the others in that he proposed to let the boys travel by bicycle. In the past, bikes had been forbidden during term time, except in the case of a few day boys who used their machines to travel to and from school. This term, however, the headmaster had relaxed his ban, and a number of boarders had taken advantage of this concession and brought their bicycles with them when they returned to school after the Easter holidays.

Jennings was one of the few who had not done so. He had quite outgrown the small machine on which he had learned to ride some years before, and he was hopefully awaiting a new and larger model which his kindly, but absent-minded, Aunt Angela had suggested as a Christmas present ... But Christmas had come and gone six months ago, and Aunt Angela, true to her reputation, had forgotten all about the gift she had promised her nephew.

Not that he had given up hope! No doubt an opportunity would arise, sooner or later, of reminding her of her promise.

So far the lack of a machine had not worried him unduly, for the other boys had had little chance of using their bicycles in the few weeks since the summer term had begun. Indeed, the proposed outing of the Natural History Club was really the cyclists' first worthwhile opportunity for an excursion awheel.

A hint that something sensational was in the wind was broadcast by Atkinson as he came bursting into Dormitory Four the following evening.

"Hey, get a move on, you lot," he panted to his colleagues who were undressing in a leisurely manner. "I've just seen Mr Carter. He's got something fantastic to tell us, if we're all in bed when he comes round."

"Nearly ready," Darbishire sang out from the washbasins. "I've just got to finish my teeth and do my famous gear-changing gargle."

"There's no time for gear-changing gargles! He'll be here in two bats of an eyelid," Atkinson went on excitedly. "And for goodness' sake put your toothbrush away. You won't have any teeth *left* if you go on scraping them much longer."

Spurred on by the fear of missing something, the five members of Dormitory Four hurried through the tedious process of washing, and were sitting up in bed by the time Mr Carter made his entrance a few minutes later.

"I'm going to give you a chance to extend your natural history researches farther afield," he told them. "So on Saturday week we shall take a picnic lunch and go and explore the river valley near Dunhambury."

Dormitory Four bounced up and down on their beds, dragging the neatly tucked sheets and blankets into a crumpled heap.

"Terrific, sir! Just the place for bird-watching!" crowed Venables. "We might even be able to do some grass-snake-spotting and hedgehog-tracking, too!"

"Hope we get something good to eat," said Temple, to whom food was always a matter of some importance.

Matron had come into the room just in time to hear the announcement. She was young and cheerful, and willing as a rule to help and sympathise with those in trouble. For this reason she was liked by all the boys, who looked upon her as a staunch ally in times of adversity.

Mr Carter smiled as he turned towards her and said, "You're the expert on school food, Matron. Have you any ideas on the subject of picnics?"

"I certainly have," she replied with mock solemnity. "Rule number one is never let boys carry their own sand-wiches. Last time we had a picnic, Jennings and Darbishire

21

had eaten the whole of their lunch and tea before they'd even left the premises."

"Oh, Matron!" Darbishire protested.

"The best plan is obviously to take all the food in one large hamper and give it out when you get there."

"We can't carry a large hamper on bicycles," Mr Carter pointed out. "I shall have to ask Mr Wilkins to come along and take the provisions in his car."

Jennings resisted the temptation to say that they would all be dead from starvation by the time Mr Wilkins' car arrived on the scene. Instead he asked, "What's all this about bikes, sir?"

"Well, it's too long a journey to undertake on foot," Mr Carter explained. "So I'm afraid this excursion will have to be confined to those of you who own bicycles."

A worried look came into Jennings' eyes. "What happens if you haven't got a bike?" he demanded.

"In that case I'm afraid you won't be able to go."

"Oh, *sir!*" Panic and alarm spread across Jennings' features. "But I *must* go, sir. I'm Chief Frog Spotter. Besides, I *have* got a bike – almost. What I mean is I haven't got it yet, but it's been promised since last Christmas."

"A fat lot of good that is," said Atkinson unsympathetically. "You'll have to stay behind, that's all. It's just your bad luck."

Jennings refused to accept defeat. "Sir, please, sir, do you think if I wrote and reminded my aunt, she'd send it in time for the picnic, sir?"

That was a question Mr Carter couldn't answer. "I've really no idea. It's a matter between you and your aunt."

Matron was quick to notice the boy's anxiety and did her best to cheer him up. "I shouldn't start worrying yet,

Jennings," she advised. "Even if the bicycle doesn't arrive, there's still a chance that you could beg a lift. If Mr Wilkins is going to take the hamper in his car he's certain to have a spare seat to offer."

Jennings' gloom deepened. There might be quite a number of non-cyclists hoping for a lift, and there was small chance that Mr Wilkins would give a seat in his car to one who had recently passed unflattering comments about it. Matron didn't know *that*, of course. If she had done so, Jennings reminded himself, she would never have made such a wildly impossible suggestion.

For some time after Mr Carter had called silence and gone downstairs to supper, Jennings lay awake pondering the problem that faced him.

The first thing to do, he decided, was to see Mr Wilkins and ask him very politely for a lift in his car. There was always a chance that he had forgotten about overhearing the flippant remarks a few days before. And just in case he *hadn't* forgotten, it would be as well to send a letter to Aunt Angela straight away. He couldn't very well ask her outright to send him a bicycle, but he could drop hints – fairly strong hints they would have to be, of course, but not so obvious that she would take umbrage and ignore his request altogether.

From there he went on to conjure up a picture of the bicycle he hoped she would buy for him. He could see it in his mind's eye as clearly as though he was looking at a glossy coloured catalogue sent free on request by the manufacturer. The machine would be a sports model with dropped handle-bars, streamlined plastic mud-guards, a dynamo lighting set and a couple of chromium-plated drinking flasks on the handle-bars.

Strictly speaking, of course, the drinking flasks were intended for racing cyclists competing in strenuous events like the Tour de France. Still, they'd come in handy on the half-mile ride to Linbury village when the weather was warm! It would be a red bicycle, he decided – a gleaming scarlet which sparkled in the sunlight. Or should it be blue? ... Yes, on second thoughts, perhaps blue would be better! Or what about green?

He had still not made up his mind about the colour when he drifted off to sleep a few minutes later.

Chapter 3

Jennings Makes Amends

The next morning after breakfast Jennings approached Mr Wilkins and made his request.

"Sir! Mr Wilkins, sir, may I ask you something, please, sir?" he began in the shy and respectful tones he kept for occasions of this kind.

Mr Wilkins paused in the act of pinning up a list on the hall notice-board.

"I'm listening," he said without enthusiasm.

"Well, sir, it's about the picnic on Saturday week, sir. I may have my bicycle by then, but if it hasn't come would you – er – could you – that is, I wondered if you'd very kindly take me in your car, sir."

The master's first impulse was to say, "Yes, I expect so."

Then he remembered! Assuming an expression of disapproval he said, "No, I don't think I will, Jennings. I seem to remember I had to speak to you only last week for trying to be funny at my expense."

"Oh, but that was just an accident, sir. I didn't know you were listening – I mean . . ."

"If you think, Jennings," Mr Wilkins said severely, "that you can make facetious remarks about my car and then calmly expect me to give you lifts all round the country-side, you – you – well, you'd better start thinking again."

Jennings thought again. First he went and found Darbishire and asked his advice about what he should say in his letter to his Aunt Angela.

"I want to sort of remind her of what she promised, without actually asking for it," he explained as they sat down at a table in the common-room.

"Yes, you don't want to overdo things," Darbishire agreed. "My father says, 'He who asks, doesn't get.' "

"That's all very well," grumbled Jennings as he opened his writing pad. "But it doesn't allow for people who are so amazingly absent-minded that they say they'll give you something and then forget all about it."

Darbishire fingered his chin, tugging at an imaginary beard – a gesture which, he claimed, helped him to think more clearly. Finally he said, "Atkinson's father gave him a bike for Christmas. You could mention that in an off-hand sort of way. It might charge your aunt's brain cells up a few amps."

"That's not a bad idea," Jennings agreed. He wiped the congealed ink from his nib with his handkerchief and set to work.

"And after that you could say . . ."

"Don't natter, Darbi. Can't you see I'm trying to write a letter?"

Ten minutes later, as the bell was ringing for morning

assembly, he laid down his pen and passed the letter across for Darbishire's approval.

"Dear Aunt Angela," Darbishire read aloud.

"I hope you are quite well. I am quite well and having good weather. On Saturday week we are all going on a picnic, but I am not as I have not got a bicycle. There is a boy named Atkinson who got a bicycle for a Christmas present, so he can go but not me, as you have to have a bicycle. It is a long time since Christmas. I hope you enjoyed the card with the robin on that I sent you. Almost everybody has a bicycle, except me, it is good exercise. I expect they will all enjoy the picnic, except me. It would be nice to go as I am Chief Frog Spotter, but you can't go if you haven't got a bike.

With love from
John."

"D'you think she'll get it?" Jennings inquired anxiously.

"Of course she'll get it – if you put a stamp on and post it, that is."

"No, you clodpoll. I mean do you think she'll see the point?" Jennings persisted. "I didn't like to make it too obvious, you see; that's why I've only dropped a veiled hint here and there among the rest of the news."

Darbishire considered the matter. "I should send it just as it is," he advised. "If she reads it carefully she may see what you're driving at. Of course, it might help if you drew a picture of everybody starting off on their bikes, and you watching them with a sad look on your face. And then you could draw a delivery van with a bicycle in . . ."

"This is supposed to be a letter, not a comic strip!"

Jennings pointed out tersely. "All I can do is to post it right away and keep my fingers crossed till she sends me an answer."

There was no letter from Aunt Angela in the week that followed. And on Thursday, two days before the picnic, Jennings gave up all hope of his bicycle arriving in time.

"It wouldn't matter so much, if only Old Wilkie would give me a lift in his car," he confided to Darbishire as they made their way upstairs to the library after lunch. "I wish I'd never said all those things about it – not when he was listening, anyway."

Darbishire was inclined to take a more optimistic view. "Don't you think he might change his mind if you were really polite to him between now and Saturday?" he suggested. "You know – opening the door for him, and passing the bread without being asked, and all that sort of thing."

Jennings looked doubtful. "I could try," he said.

"Unless, of course, your famous bike comes in the mean time," Darbishire amended. "You could stop being polite to him then."

"Yes, of course. Sheer waste of politeness," Jennings agreed, perching himself uncomfortably on the corner of the library table. "All the same, we ought to think of something better than just being polite. You could pass Sir the bread till he was bursting with the stuff, and I bet he'd never even notice you were trying to be polite."

"Well, you think of something better, then."

For some moments they thought in silence. Then Jennings jumped to his feet, smiting himself on the brow as a sign of inspiration.

"I've got it!" he cried excitedly. "I'll clean his car for him!"

Darbishire was dumbfounded with admiration for this masterly plan. A real stroke of genius, if ever he'd heard one! When speech returned, he said, "Why, yes, of course! He couldn't very well refuse to take you when you'd been to all that trouble specially for him."

"That's what I thought," Jennings replied. He breathed on his finger-nails and polished them on the lapel of his jacket as a sign that these flashes of inspiration came easily to the mind of Jennings, J. C. T. "He'd see I was really trying to make up for all those things I'd said about his rotten old – er – about his car."

He would keep his intentions secret, he decided – except from Darbishire, of course, who would have to help him to carry them out. In that way the full force of his selfless devotion to Mr Wilkins would burst upon the master as a wonderful surprise.

With a slight effort of the imagination, Jennings could visualise the scene outside the garage as Mr Wilkins prepared to set forth upon the excursion: his exclamations of delight as his eye fell upon the polished chromium and gleaming bodywork; his look of bewilderment as he wondered who had been to such trouble on his behalf . . . And then, the hearty invitation to climb aboard as he, Jennings, standing at a respectful distance, modestly admitted that he was responsible for the car's astounding transformation.

"That's settled, then. We'll do it tomorrow during break – just you and me," Jennings announced. "If we make a good job of it, it'll put him in such a good mood that he can't possibly refuse to give me a lift."

If the plan was to succeed, the first thing to do was to collect some cleaning materials, Jennings decided. So when the bell rang for break the following morning, he hurried upstairs to Dormitory Four while Darbishire kept watch on the landing in case Matron should chance to pass that way.

A rapid tour of the wash-basins furnished Jennings with all the equipment that he needed. Then the two boys slipped quietly down the back stairs and outside to the garage. Access was easy as the doors were ill-fitting and could not be locked. A minute later they were hard at work.

The task was harder than they had expected. To begin with they found to their dismay that there was no water laid on in the garage.

"What are we going to do, then?" lamented Darbishire.

"We'll have to get it out of the car, that's all," Jennings said with a shrug. He unscrewed the radiator cap and dangled his makeshift cleaning cloth inside. Even so, the remedy was not a complete success, for his efforts to wash the bonnet with insufficient water spread a pattern of muddy streaks and smears all over its surface.

"It looks more like a stripy tiger than a car at the moment," Darbishire criticised.

"Give me a chance, I haven't finished yet," Jennings replied curtly. "And anyway, how about you doing something instead of standing there like a spare dinner moaning at other people."

For some minutes they worked in silence. Then Jennings said, "Put some more elbow grease into it, Darbi! You haven't got the door handle nearly clean enough yet."

"I flipping well have!" returned Darbishire, who by this time had climbed into the car and was kneeling on the driving seat dusting the inside of the windscreen. "Look at all this dirt that's come off on Venables' face flannel."

"That was off the radiator," Jennings argued. "You've hardly touched the . . ."

He broke off in wild alarm as the raucous blare of the horn shattered the peace and quiet of the garage. Darbishire, too, leapt like a startled faun, his hand flying to his mouth in guilty realisation that he was the cause of the commotion. He must have accidentally pressed the horn button with his elbow, he thought; and now, to his horror, he found that the button had become wedged in its socket, so that the horn went on blaring its high-pitched note like a fire alarm.

"Turn it off! Turn it off! Stop it for goodness' sake!" Jennings had to shout to make himself heard.

"I can't! It won't stop!" Darbishire wailed, trying vainly to release the horn button from its socket.

In the close confines of the garage the noise was deafening. Panic seized Darbishire. He flung out his arms in a gesture of despair and caught his knuckles on one of the knobs on the dashboard. At once the windscreen wipers started swinging to and fro. After describing a few arcs, the offside wiper developed a mechanical defect and, dropping down from the windscreen, began sweeping a segment of the bonnet. . . . And all the while the shriek of the horn went blaring on at full volume.

It was Jennings who saved the situation. Flinging open the near-side door he jumped into the passenger seat and hit the steering wheel a resounding blow with his fist. Immediately, the horn button sprang back and the noise ceased.

"Phew! That was frantic!" gasped Darbishire.

31

Jennings was furious. "This is supposed to be a *secret* operation!" he stormed. "What d'you want to go and make all that row for!" He fumbled with the knob on the dashboard and the windscreen wipers came to rest.

"Sorry, Jen," Darbishire apologised. "Only you told me to polish harder."

"That doesn't mean polish louder. Anybody might have heard."

For some seconds they remained still, listening intently for the sound of approaching footsteps ... But all was quiet outside the garage, and after a few agonised moments Jennings breathed again. "Come on, then, let's get on with it," he said.

"Righto." There came a tearing sound as Darbishire, alighting from the driving seat, caught the hem of his trousers on a broken spring protruding through the upholstery.

He shook his head sadly as he inspected the damage. It was always the same, he reflected: whenever he agreed to help Jennings carry out some plan it was always he, C. E. J. Darbishire, who suffered more misfortune than anybody else.

"It's about time this old bone-shaker had a good clean up, if you ask me," Jennings observed, as he moved behind the car and began dusting the rear number plate with Bromwich's bath towel. "You should have seen Temple's nail-brush when I'd finished doing the spokes on the spare wheel."

"I know. Venables' sponge was just the same," Darbishire replied. "Still, I've nearly finished my bit now. How are you getting on?"

"I'm just going to clean the exhaust pipe." Discarding the bath towel, Jennings screwed his handkerchief into a pad and began polishing vigorously.

Darbishire sauntered round to the rear of the car to inspect his friend's labours. "I don't think you need polish the *inside* of the pipe, Jen," he remarked. "Old Wilkie isn't going to look in there."

Jennings snorted. "Listen, Darbi, when I do a job I like to do it properly!" So saying, he pushed his handkerchief a few inches farther into the interior of the exhaust pipe – so far, in fact, that he couldn't quite reach it with his fingers when he tried to extract it a few moments later.

"Oh, fish-hooks! Now look what's happened," he lamented. "I shall have to get a stick or a piece of wire or something to . . ."

He broke off as he heard his name being called in the distance. Cautiously, he tiptoed across to the garage door and peered out. Atkinson was trotting down the path, bowling imaginary in-swingers and calling Jennings' name between each delivery. He stopped in mid-action as he saw the dust-streaked face peering round the garage door.

"Oh, there you are, Jen," he said. "Mr Carter told me to tell you there's a letter for you. Venables has got it in the common-room."

"A letter! Fantastic! D'you hear that, Darbi? I bet it's from Aunt Angela. Hey, I hope it's about my bike."

Heedless of the unfinished task, and forgetting all about the handkerchief still jammed in the exhaust pipe, Jennings rushed off towards the main buildings to claim his long-awaited letter.

Darbishire pulled a long face as he watched him go.

"Tut! There you are, you see! It's always *me* who gets left with the clearing up to do," he complained. "Nobody else gets all the rotten jobs. Take Jennings, for instance: he just stonks around flipping a duster and expects me to . . ."

"What's going on, anyway?" Atkinson wanted to know.

"We've been cleaning Sir's car to put him in a good mood. You might give me a hand clearing up the mess."

"Righto." Atkinson picked up a dirty piece of cloth from the bonnet. "You don't want this chunk of oily rag, do you? Might as well chuck it away."

"No, don't do that," Darbishire warned him. "It's somebody's face flannel."

"Eh?" Atkinson peered at the grimy name-tape. "Hey, it's *mine*!" he shouted indignantly. "Coo, what cheek! Who gave you permish to . . ."

"It's all right. It'll wash off," Darbishire assured him. "Oh, yes, and you'll find Jennings' handkerchief bunged in the exhaust pipe. You might get it out, if you're cleaning up around those regions."

Unfortunately, Atkinson's efforts to remove the

handkerchief merely succeeded in pushing it farther into the pipe.

"It's no good. I can't reach it at all now," he announced after some seconds of vain poking. "It's jammed solid, about six inches down."

"Wow! Whatever shall we do, then?"

"Jennings will have to get a new one, that's all."

"I didn't mean that," Darbishire said in worried tones. "I meant what's Old Wilkie going to say?"

"He won't even know it's there. It doesn't show."

"No, but – well, you don't think it'll do the car any harm, do you?"

"I shouldn't think so." Atkinson slipped his face flannel into his pocket and turned to leave the garage. "After all, there's so much the matter with Sir's creaking old crock, anyway, that I can't see a chunk of rag in the exhaust pipe making much difference one way or the other."

Venables and Bromwich were changing the leaves in one of the caterpillar boxes when Jennings burst into the common-room.

"Atki says you've got a letter for me, Venables," he panted. "May I have it, please? It may be urgent."

"Coming over by air-mail!" With a flick of his wrist Venables sent the envelope skimming across the room, and as Jennings bent to pick it up he recognised the writing on the envelope.

It was from Aunt Angela – there was no doubt about it. But supposing she hadn't understood his carefully phrased hints? Supposing the letter ignored the whole question of bicycles, or, worse still, supposing it was to say that she had changed her mind about giving him one? Supposing . . .?

"Well, open it if you're going to," said Venables, curious to know the contents. "Thought you said it was urgent."

"So it is: it's about my bike. I was just – er – I was just . . ." Jennings tore open the envelope and scanned the single sheet of notepaper folded inside. He knew it might take him some time to decipher, for Aunt Angela's writing was extremely difficult to read – a hasty, illegible scrawl which could be solved only by a mixture of guesswork and concentration.

"What's it say?" demanded Bromwich, edging forward in an interested manner.

Jennings blinked at the scrawl and read aloud: "Dear John, I am most awfully sorry . . ."

"Oh, bad luck. So she's not going to give you one after all," Venables sympathised.

"Don't interrupt," Jennings said curtly. He went on reading: "I am most awfully sorry that I have been so long in *something the something* . . ."

He screwed up his eyes, straining to decipher the hiero-glyphics. "Her writing's terribly difficult. It looks like 'been so long in burying the bucketful'."

"Can't be. Doesn't make sense," Venables decided. "What would your aunt want to bury a bucketful of? And why should she write and . . . Here, let me have a look." Peering over Jennings' shoulder and breathing heavily down his neck, Venables sought to make sense of the puzz-ling phrase. "H'm. I think it's 'burning the binnacle'," he decided, at length. "Yes, that's what it is."

"But that doesn't make sense, either," Jennings pro-tested, laying the sheet of notepaper down on the common-room table.

"Oh, I think it does. Obviously your aunt must have

had a binnacle – whatever that is – lying about the house, and she thought it was high time it was – er – well – er . . ."

"You both need your heads seen to," said Bromwich, who had picked up the letter and was now studying it through a small magnifying-glass. "What it says is, 'have been so long in buying the bicycle'."

"Eh! Wow, yes, you're right. Good old Bromo!" Jennings crowed in glee. Eagerly he read on: " 'buying the bicycle that I promised you last Christmas lollipops.' "

"Christmas *what*?"

"Oh, sorry. Christmas *holidays* – that's what it is. Tut! Why don't they teach grown-ups to write so people can read it." He frowned over the next line and said, "This bit looks like 'your hatter swerved to jog my fairy melody'."

Venables looked puzzled. "I didn't know you'd got a hatter, Jen."

"Neither did I. Nor a fairy melody, either."

Bromwich produced his magnifying-glass. "I've got it," he said. " 'Your letter served to jog by failing memory. But I have now remembered the onion . . .' "

"What?"

"Sorry. 'I have now remedied the omission and have despatched the mac . . . mac . . . mac-*something*.' "

"Mackintosh?" queried Jennings.

"Mackerel?" hazarded Venables.

With his shoulders hunched in a scholarly stoop Bromwich continued to peer through his magnifying-glass like an archaeologist trying to decipher marks on a fragment of ancient Roman pottery. "Looks like *hine*," he said at length. "H-i-n-e. Can't be though, can it! Mac . . . *hine*. There's no such word."

"Machine!" Jennings shouted at the top of his voice.

He snatched the letter and managed to finish reading the sentence without further setback. ". . . despatched the machine-which should reach you on Friday.' "

For a moment he was too overjoyed to speak. Then, with a full-throated "Yippee!" he seized Venables and propelled him round the table in a clumsy dance.

"Friday – that's today! It'll be here this afternoon!" Jennings warbled in a shrill falsetto as though providing a vocal accompaniment to the dance.

"All right, keep calm," protested Venables, freeing himself from the clutching embrace. "No point in getting excited till you've actually seen the thing. For all you know it may be some tinny old rattletrap that'll drop to bits the first time you ride it."

"It flipping well won't," said Jennings warmly. Giving full reign to his imagination, he went on: "It'll be a super racing model with dynamo lighting, and perhaps even chromium-plated drinking flasks on the handle-bars. . . . You just wait till you see it!"

Chapter 4

A Case of Obstruction

All through afternoon school Jennings was unable to keep his mind on his work, and more than once he was taken to task by Mr Wilkins for letting his attention wander. The closing minutes of the last lesson tried his patience sorely, for it was then that he heard the rumble of a delivery van crossing the playground on its way to the kitchen yard.

Would Mr Wilkins *never* stop talking, he wondered. Would the bell *never* go? A moment later his wish was granted with the sounding of the bell, and Jennings rushed out of the room as soon as the class was dismissed.

"Come on, Darbi, and you other blokes," he shouted over his shoulder as he made for the door. "My bike's come. At least, I hope it has."

A small group of interested spectators followed him out of the room and down the stairs.

"You'll look a bit silly if it *hasn't*," Venables observed. "All that guff you gave us this morning about chromium-plated sprockets and jet-propelled pedals – not to mention aluminium hot water bottles."

"I said drinking flasks – not hot water bottles!"

"Same thing. Anyway, from the way you were swanking about it, it ought to be something worth seeing."

As he led the way through the side door leading to the kitchen yard, Jennings almost collided with the van man who came staggering in at that moment with a small crate of china on his shoulder. Anxious to know at once what further goods were waiting to be unloaded, the boy said, "Good afternoon! My name's Jennings."

"Eh?" The driver deposited the crate inside the doorway with a slight thud.

"I said my name is Jennings."

"Well, what of it?" the driver demanded, panting heavily from his exertions. "My name's Archie Cronk, but I don't go about broadcasting it at the top of my voice."

"You don't understand. What I mean is, have you got a bicycle?"

"Yes, I have, as it happens, but I don't see that it's any of your business," the van man replied. "Had it since I was a lad. Bit rusty now, of course, but it suits me well enough."

Jennings choked back his exasperation and tried again. "I mean, have you got a bicycle for me on the van? Jennings, the name is."

"Oh, I see. Yes, there is a bike on board for some such name as that. Hang on while I take this crate along to the pantry and I'll get it off for you."

But Jennings was far too impatient to cool his heels on the doorstep waiting for A. Cronk, Esq. He would go and wait by the van, he decided. In that way he would at least be able to catch a glimpse of the eagerly awaited machine.

Surrounded by his jostling swarm of colleagues, he hurried out into the kitchen yard. But Venables, who was already in the lead, broke into a run and reached the van some yards ahead of the others.

"Is it there?" Jennings called as he came scampering up to join him.

By way of reply Venables let forth a yell of derisive laughter. "It's come all right," he shouted back. "Wait till you see it!" Whereupon, he dissolved into peals of mirth, doubling himself up and sagging at the knees in helpless hilarity.

"What's the joke?" Jennings demanded curtly. "I can't see anything funny in . . ."

The words froze to silence as he reached the rear end of the van and looked inside. For there, propped up against a stiff roll of wire-netting near the tail-board, was a two-wheeled vehicle that was, undoubtedly, a bicycle. But what caused him to gape in wide-eyed dismay was the fact that the machine was not a new one. The mudguards were bent, the paintwork scratched, the saddle sagged and two spokes were missing from the back wheel.

He could hardly believe his eyes. Never, for one moment, had he thought that Aunt Angela would send him a *second-hand* machine. His dreams of a gleaming new sports model dissolved in a flash as he stood numb with disappointment, listening to the jeering comments going on around him.

"Wow! What a rotten old tank engine!" squawked Temple. "It's even older than Old Wilkie's car."

"Serves you right for swanking!" said Bromwich. "All that eye-wash about your supersonic new bike, and it's only a prehistoric knife-grinding contraption after all."

"I bet it'll conk out on the way to the picnic," prophesied Atkinson, damp-eyed with mirth. He danced round the unhappy Jennings, flapping his fingers and pulling idiotic faces in wild derision. "Honk, honk!" he shouted. "Make way for Jennings on his jet-propelled fire-escape!"

Others joined in the pantomime, and for some moments Jennings was the centre of a gibbering circle of mocking, cat-calling dancers. After a while this exercise began to pall, and the interested spectators, still weak with laughter, ran off to spread the news of his disappointment round the school.

Only Darbishire remained. He had taken no part in the jeering demonstration which had shocked his feelings of fair play. Now he said, "Bad luck, Jen."

Jennings didn't reply at once. He was disappointed, of course, but even in his disappointment he absolved Aunt Angela from blame. After all, it was good of her to give him a bicycle of *any* sort – even one that fell so far short of his expectations. It wasn't fair to blame her for the fact that her well-meaning efforts would make him the laughing stock of the school.

He shrugged his shoulders and forced a wan smile. "Can't be helped," he said. He reached up over the tailboard with the intention of lifting the bicycle down from the van. At the same moment he heard footsteps behind him, followed by the fruity tones of Archibald Cronk.

"Hey, what are you up to, son?"

Somewhat guiltily Jennings withdrew his hands. "I was just going to get my bike down off the van," he explained.

"*Your* bike! What d'you mean, *your* bike? That's *my* bike, when you've quite finished lugging it about."

Jennings stared at the van man in perplexity. "But you said you'd brought one for me. You said it was on the van."

"So it is, but it ain't *this* one," replied Mr Cronk, heaving himself up over the tail-board. "This here is my bike, see. I take it round in the van on the afternoon delivery, so I can ride home from the depot, see."

"Then you mean . . ." A faint hope glimmered in Jennings' mind: a hope that became stronger as Mr Cronk disappeared into the gloom at the far end of the van. There came a slight bumping as of parcels being shifted, and then he picked his way back to the tail-board, half-pushing and half-carrying a shiny new bicycle.

"Here you are, son. This is the one you want," he said, lowering it down to the ground. "I'll get you to sign for it. Hang on while I find my delivery notes."

Jennings was too overcome to speak. He stood holding the bicycle by the handle-bars and staring at it in a trance of delight. Coming so soon after his disappointment he seemed almost unable to believe his stroke of good fortune. Still in a daze, he scribbled his name on the delivery note and watched the van drive slowly out of the kitchen yard.

"Wow! Isn't it super!" gasped Darbishire for the tenth time as the van disappeared from view. "Aren't you going to take the wrappings off so you can see it properly?"

Jennings came out of his trance and switched on a wide smile of pure joy. "Yes, of course, Darbi. Good old Aunt Angela. I might have known she wouldn't let me down. She's OK, really."

The machine, stripped of its protective wrappings, was everything that he could wish for. To begin with, it was a make of which he approved and was just the right size for his height. The frame was enamelled a shiny royal blue and the mudguards were white, while a small union jack attached to the lamp bracket added a further touch of gaiety to the colour scheme. Admittedly there was no dynamo lighting set, nor yet a pair of aluminium drinking flasks, but after all, what did that matter!

Now he came to think of it he didn't *really* want a dynamo, he decided; the school rules forbade cycling after dark, so an expensive form of lighting would have been a sheer waste of money anyway. And as for the drinking flasks – well, he could always quench his thirst at the nearest tap . . . Yes, his machine was easily the best in the school, he told himself. Just wait till the others saw it!

He swung his leg over the saddle and rode out of the kitchen yard with Darbishire trotting at his heels.

By this time a somewhat confusing description of the new bicycle was being broadcast throughout the school by the interested spectators. On the playground Temple and Atkinson were entertaining Binns and Blotwell with an eye-witness account of its arrival.

"I was one of the first to see it," Temple was saying. "Honestly, you never saw such a gruesome old gridiron. It's about a hundred years old and it's got square wheels."

"You should have seen old Jennings' face when he saw it," added Atkinson. "He nearly had a fit. And the funny part is he's been telling everyone what a supersonic, brand-new streamlined model it was going to . . ."

The words faltered to a stop as Jennings cycled round the corner on to the playground and came heading towards the group at a brisk 12 mph.

Temple's jaws dropped through a sharp angle and his eyes opened wide. Atkinson's mouth, already open in speech, remained ajar in sheer astonishment.

"Wow! Wherever did you get that from, Jen?" Temple gasped out.

"It's a present from my aunt," said Jennings airily, braking the machine to a halt. "What are you looking so fossilised about? You were there when the van man brought it, weren't you?"

"Yes, but . . ."

"Why, it's a really great bike," shrilled Binns. "You must be up the pole, Atki, telling us what a chronic old ruin it was."

"Did he tell you that?" Jennings inquired with feigned surprise.

"Yes, he did. Honestly! So did Temple," squeaked Blotwell, pointing an indignant finger at the bearers of false tidings.

"You don't want to pay any attention to uncivilised specimens like Temple and Atkinson," Jennings said solemnly. "They're always getting things round their necks." With a withering glance at the false prophets, he mounted his bicycle and pedalled off on a demonstration circuit round the playground.

That evening, Jennings wrote his "thank you" letter to Aunt Angela. And the following morning he spent every spare moment riding his bicycle round and round the playground.

"If I'd known it was coming, I wouldn't have wasted all that time cleaning Old Wilkie's car," he remarked to Darbishire during a pause between circuits. "Sheer waste of energy, that was, seeing that I don't need a lift after all."

"Oh, I don't know! It'll probably put him in a good mood for the picnic," Darbishire replied.

At Mr Carter's request, Form Three had been granted

leave of absence from the last lesson of the morning, so that they could reach their destination in time for lunch. At ten minutes to twelve they hurried out of class and fetched their machines from the bicycle shed.

Jennings was the first to reach the playground, and while he waited for the others to arrive he continued to ride round and round like a competitor in a six-day bicycle race. On his third lap he heard Matron calling to him from an upstairs window, so he dismounted, leaving his machine against the wall, and hurried across to hear what she had to say.

"Would you like to take the food for the picnic along to Mr Wilkins' garage for me?" she called down to him from a dormitory window.

"Yes, rather, Matron."

"It's all packed up in a laundry basket. You'll find it at the end of the corridor on the . . ."

"All right, Matron. I'll get it." In his eagerness to help, he rushed indoors without giving her a chance to finish her instructions.

Outside the linen-room on the first landing, he spied a medium-sized laundry basket. This must be the one, he decided without bothering to investigate the contents. After all, had not Matron told him that it was ready and waiting. Seizing one of the handles, he began sliding the heavy hamper along the landing. At the top of the stairs he met Temple hurrying out of the common-room with a butterfly net.

"Hey, give me a hand with this lot," Jennings sang out. "It's the food for the picnic. Old Wilkie's waiting for it."

"Righto!" Temple grasped the other handle, and

between them they bumped the hamper down the stairs and carried it out through the side door.

"Wow! It's really heavy," Temple observed. "D'you think Sir's springs will be all right?"

"I shouldn't think his car has *got* any springs," said Jennings. "What worries me is whether the creaking old gridiron will get there before lighting-up time."

As they approached the garage they saw half a dozen members of the Natural History Club grouped round the entrance, wearing anxious expressions on their faces. From within came the continuous grinding of a self-starter vainly trying to infuse a spark of life into a dead engine.

"There's been a catastrophe. Old Wilkie's car won't go," Venables informed them gloomily. "He and Mr Carter have been bashing away at it for the last five minutes. It just goes *a-junka-junka-junka* and then stops again."

"Wow! That's serious!" said Jennings, setting the basket down heavily on Temple's left foot. "Anyway, let's get ye provisions stowed aboard for a kick-off. Come on, Temple, one, two, three, *heave*!"

Between them the two boys swung the basket into the open boot of the car. It landed with a thud that set the vehicle bouncing on its springs and caused Mr Wilkins to shoot his head out of the driving seat window to see what was happening. His temper, already ruffled by the events of the past few minutes, was not improved when Jennings said brightly, "Won't it start, sir?"

"Don't ask such stupid questions, you silly little boy!" Mr Wilkins replied testily. "You don't imagine I'm sitting here pressing the starter just for the fun of the thing, do you?"

Mr Wilkins' head shot out of the window.

Mr Carter's head emerged from beneath the open bonnet. "I can find nothing wrong with the engine, Wilkins," he reported. "I just don't understand it at all."

"But this is ridiculous. It's never behaved like this before," Mr Wilkins grumbled as he climbed out of the driving seat and stood scratching his head in perplexity.

"Perhaps it's just old age, sir," suggested Darbishire. "After all, there must come a time when . . ." He stopped abruptly on catching sight of Mr Wilkins' smouldering expression. "Sorry, sir," he mumbled and blew his nose to cover his confusion.

It was this action that caused Jennings to remember his own handkerchief firmly wedged in the exhaust pipe. In his excitement at the arrival of his bicycle he had completely forgotten about that trifling mishap. Now, the thought of it made him feel vaguely uneasy. Could *that* be the cause of the trouble? It was possible, to say the least; and though he did not relish the thought of explaining matters to the indignant Mr Wilkins, he realised that the situation would have to be faced.

"Sir, please, sir! I *think* I know what might be wrong," he began.

"Be quiet, Jennings," Mr Wilkins said irritably. "Mr Carter and I have got quite enough on our hands without listening to your idiotic prattle."

"But I'm almost sure I know what it is, sir," Jennings persisted. "If you got a piece of wire you could hoik it out of the exhaust pipe quite easily, sir, and then the car would . . ."

"Are you trying to be funny?"

"No, sir, honestly."

It was Mr Carter who deduced from the boy's earnest

tone that there might be something more than met the eye in this unlikely theory. Accordingly, he made his way to the rear of the car and knelt down to investigate.

"By jove, he's right, Wilkins. There *is* something in the exhaust," he exclaimed. "Here, pass me those pliers, Venables."

A few moments later the crumpled rag had been extracted. "Now try it, Wilkins," Mr Carter advised.

At the first push of the starter the engine roared to life. Gasps of joy and sighs of relief arose from the members of the Natural History Club. Now, at any rate, there would be no lack of transport for the picnic basket.

"No wonder we were having trouble," Mr Carter said with a smile.

"Why, sir, what was wrong?" demanded Venables.

"I should have thought it was obvious. An engine won't go unless the burnt-out gases can escape through the exhaust pipe."

"And it was all due to Jennings that we found out, wasn't it, sir?" Bromwich said generously. "He guessed what was wrong in a flash, didn't he!"

"He certainly did!" Mr Wilkins beamed a smile of gratitude in the boy's direction. "Well done, Jennings! You seem to have saved the situation."

Jennings looked down at the toes of his shoes and said nothing. Mr Carter, however, seemed more concerned with how the obstruction came to be in the exhaust pipe in the first place. He spread out the crumpled handkerchief and examined the corners until he found the name tape. "J. C. T. Jennings," he read out.

The announcement had a curious effect upon Mr Wilkins. He leaped like a startled heifer which, grazing peacefully in a field with its comrades, has carelessly walked into the electric fence.

"Eh! What's that? I – I – I . . . Did *you* put that rag in there, Jennings?" he barked.

"Yes, sir. I'm terribly sorry. I forgot to take it out, sir."

"Forgot to take it out! But what, in the name of thunder, did you want to put it *in* for, you silly little boy! You must be off your head!"

"I was cleaning it, sir. The pipe, I mean – not the handkerchief."

"*Doh!*" Mr Wilkins sawed the air as though conducting an invisible orchestra. "You've no business to go about cleaning exhaust pipes with dirty handkerchiefs!"

"It was a clean one that morning, sir."

"That's not the point. If it hadn't been discovered in time, the car wouldn't have started and the whole expedition would have been ruined. Very well, then: you will be punished for your stupid meddling and disobedience. . . . You can stay behind!"

Jennings stared at Mr Wilkins in horror and disbelief, shocked beyond measure at the severity of the punishment he had imposed.

"Oh, sir!" he gasped in dismay. "Stay *behind*, sir! Not go on the expedition at *all*!"

Chapter 5

The Picnic

Numb with disappointment, Jennings turned to leave the garage. At the door he stopped and made a final appeal.

"I was only trying to do you a favour, sir. I thought you'd be pleased if I cleaned the car for you."

"It's no good arguing, Jennings. You're not coming, and that's that," Mr Wilkins retorted, slamming down the lid of the boot. "I've had just about enough of your nonsense. If it wasn't for your stupid behaviour I'd be halfway to Dunhambury by now."

Outside the garage Jennings pouted and blew out his cheeks in frustration. "Absolutely not fair! That's the last time I'm going out of my way to do good turns for people," he muttered beneath his breath.

The members of the Natural History Club sympathised with the Chief Frog Spotter in discreet undertones.

"Bad luck, Jen," Darbishire whispered. "Never mind, though. I'll tell you all about it when we get back."

"Huh! Fat lot of comfort that is," Jennings snorted. "Besides, think of all the hoo-hah and trouble I went to in getting my new bike here in time. And now . . ." His voice faltered and he gulped slightly. "And now I'm not even allowed to use it."

Mr Wilkins reversed the car out of the garage and drove round the corner on to the playground. Having wasted so much time already he was anxious to be on his way. But, to his annoyance, a further delay awaited him. As he was crossing the playground, heading for the drive and the main gates beyond, he heard high-pitched shouts and whistles coming from behind him. A glance in the driving mirror revealed Binns and Blotwell pounding along in the rear waving their arms and calling at the tops of their voices.

"Sir! . . . Sir! . . . Stop, sir!" The shrill urgency of their tones caused the master to bring the car to a standstill and switch off the engine.

"What's the matter now?" he demanded irritably as the two boys panted to a halt beside him.

"Phew! Thank goodness we caught you, sir. We've run flat out every step of the way from Matron's room," gasped Binns. "I should think we must have done a four-minute mile in three minutes, sir."

Mr Wilkins was not interested in athletic records. "Well, go on, boy. What's it all about?"

"It's about the picnic, sir. Good job you hadn't started or there wouldn't be anything to eat when you got there, sir."

Mr Wilkins looked puzzled. "What are you talking about? I've got all the food for the picnic in the car. It's in a laundry basket in the boot."

"No, it isn't, sir," said Blotwell in gleeful triumph. "That's why we've come to stop you. Matron says you've got the wrong basket, sir. We just came out of Art to change the paint water, you see, sir, and she told us to . . ."

"Uh?" With a grunt of impatience Mr Wilkins climbed out of the car to inspect the contents of the boot. His impatience turned to surprise when, lifting the lid of the hamper, his eye fell upon a pile of clean sheets and pillow-cases.

"What – what . . . This is ridiculous!" he fumed. "I understood the food was in here. What's happened to the proper one?"

As though in answer to his query, Marshall and Petti-grew, who, as fourth-formers were not eligible to join the expedition, came out of the side door and staggered across the playground towards him with a laundry basket. In appearance, the two receptacles were identical when set down side by side, but the second one, upon inspection, proved to be full of sandwiches, buns and bottles of fizzy drinks.

"Matron only just discovered it, sir," Marshall announced. "She says she knows what must have hap-pened, but she didn't have time to explain or we should have missed you, sir."

By this time, Mr Carter had led his contingent of cyc-lists on to the playground in readiness for their journey. Observing the discussion in progress behind the stationary car, he made his way across to see what was wrong.

"There's been a bish, sir, but it's all right now," Binns greeted him.

"Yes, sir. Crisis narrowly averted," Pettigrew added with a solemn nod of the head.

The two open baskets told their own story. "H'm. Perhaps it was just as well that Jennings *did* delay you, after all, Wilkins," Mr Carter remarked.

"Don't talk to me about Jennings!" his colleague replied testily. "It was his stupid interference that nearly stopped my car from going on the picnic at all. Why, if he hadn't told us that he'd brilliantly blocked up the exhaust pipe we – we – well, we should have been sunk."

"Quite. But don't forget, Wilkins, that we should have been sunk even more deeply if you'd arrived at the picnic with nothing to offer us for lunch except clean sheets and pillow-cases!" Mr Carter pointed out. "In fact, we ought to be grateful to Jennings for those delaying tactics of his. It's entirely due to him that there'll be something to eat when we get there."

As he listened to this new aspect of the matter Mr Wilkins' expression slowly changed. "Yes, perhaps you're right, Carter," he answered thoughtfully. "I hadn't looked at it like that, to tell you the truth."

It was, perhaps, fortunate for Jennings that both the masters had been so engrossed in their efforts to start the car that they had not noticed who had been responsible for producing the wrong basket in the first place. Obviously *someone* had made a careless mistake, but this might well have been the fault of any one of the dozen or so boys clustered round the garage door. Unless they were prepared to hold an inquiry into the matter – and there seemed to be little point in such time-wasting procedure – they had no reason to connect Jennings with the blunder, any more than anyone else.

Mr Wilkins glanced at the party of cyclists eager to be on their way. Standing all alone, some distance behind the group, was a forlorn figure watching his colleagues with wistful longing.

"Come here, Jennings," Mr Wilkins called.

Moodily Jennings approached, wondering what further misfortune awaited him. Somewhat to his surprise, he found himself being addressed not as a criminal, but merely as an amiable imbecile.

"It may interest you to know, Jennings, that your unbe-lievably stupid behaviour, for which I decided to punish you a few minutes ago, has turned out to be a blessing in disguise," Mr Wilkins began.

"Yes, sir . . . No, sir . . . I beg your pardon, sir?" stammered Jennings, completely at a loss to understand what the master was talking about.

"And that being the case, I've decided to let you off your punishment. You can come on the expedition after all."

"Oh, thank you, sir! Thank you very much, sir." The sparkle came back in Jennings' eyes and he flapped his fingers in delight.

"Don't thank me – thank Mr Carter. It was he who pointed the matter out," said Mr Wilkins gruffly. Where-upon he climbed once more into the driving seat and pressed the starter.

As the car moved away in a swirl of exhaust smoke, Jennings stood staring after it, unable to believe his good fortune. He was still not quite sure why his punishment had been cancelled. But why waste time bothering about the reason? It was the outcome that mattered, and he had no cause to complain about that.

With a joyful "Yippee!" he turned and scampered across the playground to fetch his bicycle.

The river valley turned out to be an ideal place for a

nature excursion. Mr Carter had chosen a site near the market town of Dunhambury, where the valley widens and the river meanders its way down to the sea some three or four miles away.

To everyone's surprise and relief Mr Wilkins' car made the journey without mishap, and a picnic lunch was awaiting the hungry club members when they arrived.

They sat on the grass in little groups eating their sandwiches, while Mr Carter strolled about, dispensing bottles of fizzy drink and listening with half an ear to the snippets of conversation going on around him. The chief topic appeared to be the confusion caused by the identical laundry baskets.

"Yes, but what I don't understand is how all those sheets and stuff came to be in Sir's car in the first place," he heard Venables remark through a mouthful of egg sandwich.

"That was just a sort of accidental bish," replied Jennings, who had evidently given some thought to the matter during the five-mile cycle ride. "I didn't bother to look inside, you see, because Matron told me to hurry up and . . ."

Mr Carter raised one eyebrow and swivelled round in surprise.

"Jennings! Do you mean to say it was *you*, of all people, who brought the wrong basket along to the garage?"

"Yes, sir. Didn't you know, sir?"

"I certainly didn't. Neither did Mr Wilkins."

"It was just bad luck really, sir," Jennings explained. "There must have been two baskets on the landing, you see, sir – one at each end – and accidentally I . . ."

"Accidentally!" Mr Carter echoed. "Don't you realise it was for accidentally delaying the car that you were let off

57

your punishment! If Mr Wilkins had known that you were the cause of *both* accidents I'm quite sure he'd never have allowed you to come!"

"No, sir. I suppose he wouldn't." Jennings brooded over this pronouncement for a moment. Then he said, "In that case it was a really good thing I made two bishes, wasn't it, sir? They sort of cancelled each other out."

Mr Carter smiled to himself as he passed on to the next group of picnickers, where Mr Wilkins, now in an excellent humour, was entertaining the boys about him with a funny story. It was one which they had heard many times before, but they managed to raise a dutiful laugh so as not to hurt his feelings. It would be a pity, Mr Carter decided, to spoil his colleague's lunch by telling him the facts that had just come to light.

After lunch and all through the afternoon, the boys collected a wide range of plants and insects. In addition they spotted, sketched, observed, tracked, and made notes on the wildlife of the valley. Some of the observations were so improbable that the secretary refused to accept them for his Nature Diary.

"You're crazy, Atki! You couldn't possibly have heard a rattlesnake! There aren't any in this country," Darbishire protested, when asked to record Atkinson's narrow escape from a dangerous encounter.

"Well, it rattled, anyway. I heard it," Atkinson argued. "Of course, it *might* have been that box of drawing pins Bromo had in his pocket, but I still think . . ."

Darbishire snorted in disbelief and turned away to consider Bromwich's claim that he had discovered a beaver dam across the river.

"I bet it isn't. I bet it's just some ancient old branch that's fallen into the water," he decided.

In spite of some fantastic claims of this nature, a great many specimens were collected and some genuine observations made. So many, indeed, that the secretary was kept busy recording data all the afternoon, and it was not until it was nearly time to start the journey home that he had any free time to himself. At last, however, at Jennings' suggestion, he abandoned his secretarial duties and the two boys trotted off to explore a riverside copse some distance from the base camp.

"None of the other blokes have been as far as this," Jennings observed as they made their way through the undergrowth. "There's probably all sorts of things here, if only we had time to explore properly."

Soon they reached the river bank and followed it for some distance until, approaching a bend, they saw a small island in midstream.

"That'd be a good place to explore," Jennings decided. "An uninhabitable island like that is bound to be bursting with wildlife and stuff."

"Yes, of course. Just the spot for a bird sanctuary," Darbishire prattled happily. "The snag is, how could we get there? Easy enough for the birds, of course, but . . ."

He broke off as Jennings clutched his arm in sudden excitement. "What's the matter?"

By way of reply Jennings pointed to the opposite bank. They had rounded a bend by this time and there, just across the water, was a landing stage where a number of rowing boats, skiffs and punts were moored. At the head of the landing stage was a signboard. *Boats for Hire: £1 per hour*, it read.

"There you are, Darbi! That's how we could do it!" he cried in triumph.

"Go by boat! Wow, what a lobsterous wheeze!" Darbishire gazed at his friend in wide-eyed admiration. Then the practical difficulties of the plan occurred to him. "Yes, but we'd have to get permish from Mr Carter and he'd be sure to say no. The river's out of bounds, don't forget. And anyway, we're on the wrong side. We'd have to go round and . . ."

Even as he spoke the distant sound of a referee's whistle broke on the air.

"Tut! There you are. That means we've got to go back already. I knew we'd never be able to do it," he lamented.

Disappointed, they trudged their way back to join the main party. Mr Wilkins' car had already left when they arrived, and Mr Carter was assembling the cyclists for the return journey.

"Come along, you two – last as usual," he greeted them. "Hurry up and get ready: we've got to be back by six o'clock."

As he pedalled along the road on the homeward trek, Jennings' thoughts were still on the little island and the prospect of exploring it by boat.

"I'll tell you what we'll do, Darbi," he said as he rode side by side with his friend. "The very next time we come here we'll flipping well hire one of those boats."

"But there may not *be* a next time," Darbishire objected. "Mr Carter may not bring us again, and anyway, he'd never let us go on the river by ourselves."

"Then we'll flipping well go without asking. We'll fox out one half-holiday when the coast's clear, leave our bikes at the boat-house, and off we go!"

"Crystallised cheese-cakes!" Darbishire was so appalled by the boldness of the plan that he wobbled unsteadily and nearly rode into the ditch. Some people had the craziest ideas, he reflected bitterly. Take Jennings, for instance: this plan of his was simply asking for trouble. Supposing somebody saw them! . . . Supposing they were caught! . . . Supposing . . . He heaved a sigh of resignation and gave up supposing. It was useless to argue with Jennings when once his mind was made up. On the other hand, there was always the hope that they would have no chance to carry out this risky plan. So many of Jennings' brilliant brain-waves suffered this fate that there was really no point in worrying about what might never happen.

Unfortunately for Darbishire's peace of mind, Jennings' opportunity of going ahead with his scheme occurred sooner than either of them had expected.

On the following Saturday, the Linbury Court 2nd XI were due to play a home match against Bracebridge, a school not far from Dunhambury. Normally, Jennings would certainly have been selected for the team, but as luck would have it a large and painful blister appeared on his heel after cricket practice on the Wednesday afternoon. For the rest of the day he limped about in discomfort, and in the evening he reported his complaint to Matron.

"I think you'd better not play games for the rest of the week," she told him. "That'll give it a chance to heal up properly."

Jennings' first reaction was one of bitter disappointment, for he had been looking forward to the Bracebridge match. But while he was undressing in Dormitory Four that evening it occurred to him that his exclusion from the side might be made to serve a useful purpose. At any rate it was worth trying!

The list of the team was posted up on the notice-board on Thursday morning, and as soon as he had scanned the names, Jennings limped off to the common-room to find Darbishire.

"Listen, Darbi. I'm not playing on Saturday. Mr Carter's put Atkinson in the team instead of me," he announced.

"Coo! Mouldy chizz!" said Darbishire staunchly. He snorted his displeasure at a furry caterpillar in a cigar box whose antics he had been studying for the previous ten minutes. "Atki's batting is chronic, and he's about as much use at square leg as a flat-footed hedgehog, if you ask me."

"Yes, I know, but it's only because of my blister. The point is, this will give us a chance to go off and explore our island. We'll get permish to cycle down to the village, and then, instead of coming straight back, we'll beetle off to the valley."

Darbishire's heart missed a beat. "But what if someone finds out?" he demurred.

"They won't. They'll all be so busy watching the match that no one will bother about us when once it's started. It'll be all right, Darbi, don't you worry."

All day long on Friday the rain poured down in torrents. By the evening, puddles had formed all over the cricket square, and though Saturday morning dawned bright and clear, Mr Carter was doubtful whether the pitch was really fit for use. He was reluctant to cancel the match as the boys were looking forward to it eagerly, so he decided to say nothing of his fears about the state of the ground until he had made a further inspection after lunch. There was no point in dashing the hopes of the team while there was still a chance that play was possible.

Unfortunately, Jennings had no idea that the afternoon's arrangements were liable to be altered when he resolved to go ahead with his plan. At two o'clock he hustled the protesting Darbishire along to the staff-room and knocked at the door.

Mr Wilkins was the duty master that afternoon. He looked up from marking a pile of exercise books as the two boys entered.

"Sir, please, sir, may we have permish to go into Linbury on our bikes, please, sir?" Jennings asked. He made the request with a reasonably clear conscience. After all, the road to the village was the first stage of their journey. About the *second* stage he decided it would be better to say nothing.

"Yes, all right, and mind you come straight back. All boys not playing have got to watch the match," the duty master told them.

Jennings and Darbishire wasted no time. Hurrying down the stairs and out to the bicycle shed, they collected their machines and set off at once on the first lap of their secret excursion.

It was quarter past two when Mr Carter paid his visit to the headmaster's study.

"Bad news, I'm afraid, HM," he reported. "I've just had another look at the pitch. I was hoping it would be all right by this afternoon, but unfortunately it's hardly dried out at all after yesterday's rain."

"Pity! That means we shall have to cancel the match.

The boys will be disappointed." Mr Pemberton-Oakes stretched out his hand for the telephone on the desk before him. "I'd better phone up Bracebridge straight away. They'll be starting out in a few minutes if we don't stop them."

He lifted the receiver and dialled the number, noting as he did so that the sun was now shining brightly outside the window. The headmaster murmured a *tut-tut* of reproach. Of what use was the brilliant sunshine now that the pitch was waterlogged?

After a short delay, the voice of Mr Parkinson of Brace-bridge crackled over the line, and for some minutes the two headmasters discussed the difficulty that had arisen. Finally, Mr Pemberton-Oakes said, "Good idea, Parkinson! Yes, I certainly think that's the best solution. We'll bring our team over to Bracebridge, then, if you don't mind the match starting somewhat later than usual."

With a satisfied smile the headmaster replaced the receiver and turned to Mr Carter. "Parkinson says their pitch is in quite good condition, so we've arranged to play the match on their ground, instead. Unfortunately he has to go out during the afternoon, but he hopes to be back in time to see the end of the game."

"Splendid," Mr Carter agreed. "I'll go and let our boys know at once so that they can start getting ready. You'll be taking your car, I suppose, HM?"

"Yes, I can squash four in the back, provided they're not all bulky ones. And if you and Wilkins can manage the rest in your cars, that will solve the problem of transport."

"I'll see to it right away." Mr Carter strode briskly to the door, anxious to lose no time in announcing the change of plan. On the threshold he turned and said, "It should be a good match. I think we should just beat them if our lads are up to their usual form."

"Let's hope so. Still, we mustn't be over-confident," the headmaster replied. "The afternoon may yet produce an unexpected surprise."

In one respect the headmaster was right. There was certainly a surprise in store, but it had nothing to do with the laws of cricket.

Chapter 6

Collision afloat

For the first three miles, Jennings and Darbishire followed the route they had taken on the Natural History excursion the previous week. Then they made a short detour and crossed a bridge in order to reach the far side of the river.

Now that they were well away from school premises, Darbishire began to feel a little easier in his mind. After all, had not Jennings said that nothing could go wrong with his carefully devised plan? ... Very well, then. What was there to worry about!

In theory, of course, the real purpose of the expedition was to investigate the wildlife – if any – on the island they had sighted from the farther bank. But now that they were actually on their way, this aspect of the scheme seemed less important than it had done before. It was the lure of the river, and the gentle joy of messing about in a boat that mattered more than anything else.

At one point of the journey they took a wrong turning

which delayed them for some minutes, but shortly before three o'clock they reached the mooring stage and parked their bicycles against the side of the boat-house.

"I suppose it'll be safe to leave our bikes here," Jennings said doubtfully. "Pity we haven't got anything to lock them up with."

"They'll be all right. There's no one about," replied Darbishire. "Anyway, we'll just have to risk it."

"Huh! All very well for *you* risking it. Nobody would want to waltz off with your ancient old crock, anyway. But what about my new bike?"

"Why don't you get yourself a padlock then, if you're so fussy?" Darbishire answered. "As a matter of fact I saw an advertisement for some in a magazine in the library the other day. Super-looking combination padlocks, they were. Only one pound, post free."

"Sounds just right," Jennings agreed. "I think I'll write up for one. Mr Carter's still got three pounds ten pence left of my pocket money." So saying, he led the way round to the front of the boat-house and jerked his thumb at the notice-board announcing the hire of boats. "One pound an hour," he said fumbling in his pocket for the fifty pence he had brought with him. "Hand over your contribution, Darbi, and I'll go and find the boatman."

Darbishire looked blank. "*My* contribution. I thought you were paying for this. After all, it's your famous plan, isn't it?"

"Yes, I dare say, but it's only fair for you to pay half. Fifty pence each, I thought."

"Well, you're going to be unlucky. I haven't got any money on me."

Jennings stared at his friend in dismay. "Well, I like the

cheek of that! You are a swizzler, Darbi. You might have said so before."

"How was I to know? You never said anything about my paying, and anyway, you just said you'd got three pounds ten pence, so what are you worrying about?"

"I haven't got it *on* me, you clodpoll. I said it was in the school bank."

"Well, in that case you should have . . ."

"All right, all right. We'll have to make do with my fifty pence, that's all," Jennings broke in. "We'll hire the boat for half an hour instead."

By this time, the boatman, a large, sun-bronzed man in shirt-sleeves, had emerged from the boat-house and stood ready to attend to their needs. It was not usual, he explained, to let his boats out on the river for less than an hour at a time, but he was willing to make an exception in this case as the boys were obviously short of cash. He was also willing, he told them, to keep an eye on the bicycles while his customers were afloat.

Darbishire's conscience began to worry him again as the boatman was untying their craft from the mooring post.

"I'm not sure that we ought to go on with this, Jen," he said in worried tones. "What about your bad heel? Oughtn't you to be resting it?"

"Don't worry about that. It's almost better now, and anyway I don't row with my heels."

"No, but – well – suppose the Head or Old Wilkie or someone decided to come for a walk along the river?"

"How could they? They're all back at school watching the 2nd XI play Bracebridge." The information, though inaccurate, was given in good faith, and Darbishire was obliged to search his mind for some further excuse to offer.

"I'm not much good at handling boats – practically a land-lubber, you might say," he twittered nervously. "And the shipping forecast on the radio this morning was terrible. Gales in the Irish Sea, high winds off the coast of Scotland, poor visibility in . . ."

"Don't you worry, son. You'll barely get round the bend and back in half an hour – let alone row to Scotland," the boatman chimed in, as he held the boat steady for the boys to step aboard. "Now then, which of you is going to do the rowing?"

"I am," said Jennings, lurching heavily down on to the seat in a way that made the little boat rock dangerously from side to side. "It's my fifty pence, so bags I take command."

With some misgiving Darbishire stepped gingerly aboard and sat down opposite his friend. The boatman gave them a push which sent them out into midstream where, for some moments, they spun round and round in small circles, while Jennings vainly tried to bring the craft under control.

Darbishire watched his efforts with concern. As they drifted about in a haphazard fashion he said, "Hey, Jen, you're not much cop at rowing, if you don't mind my saying so."

Jennings' expression was grim and determined. "Give me a chance! I'll get the hang of it in a moment," he muttered. "After all, I've never rowed a boat before!"

"What!" Darbishire stared at his friend in blank amazement. "You mean you *can't row*! You've never driven a rowing boat before?"

"No, but I'll soon get the hang of it. Don't worry, Darbi. You just sit there and be a passenger. Leave the navigation to me."

In spite of this reassurance, the passenger refused to remain cool, calm and collected.

"Well, you've got a nerve, Jen. You invite me out on a boating expedition, and as soon as we get started you turn round and tell me . . ."

"I'm *not* turning round – it's too risky in a little boat like this," replied Jennings. "And if you go on fidgeting about like a bull on a bicycle, you'll have the boat over. For goodness' sake sit still!"

"I can't sit still, I'm too worried," Darbishire protested. "Here we are, miles from land – well, twenty yards, anyway – and neither of us knows how to manage the boat. Honestly, Jen, I've met some crazy maniacs in my time, but I reckon you take the silver medal for beetle-headed lunacy against all-comers!"

The boat had been turning round and round in small circles while Darbishire was making his protest. Now, in response to Jennings' clumsy attempts, it started drifting back towards the bank and finally bumped into the landing stage with a slight thud.

The boatman was surprised to see them again so soon. "Forgotten something?" he inquired.

"Er – well – you see . . ." Jennings racked his brain for some face-saving excuse. "What time did you say we had to bring the boat back?"

"Half past three," replied the boatman. He noticed the boy's unskilful efforts to turn the boat and added, "Two oars are a bit heavy for you, son. Why don't you take one apiece?"

The master mariner was secretly glad of this advice.

"Go on then, Darbi. You can help me row if you like," he offered.

Gingerly Darbishire took one of the oars. At any rate, he told himself, he wouldn't be any worse at it than his partner.

The boatman watched their efforts with some misgiving. If he had realised earlier that the boys were complete novices, he might have thought twice before hiring out his boat. Now, however, it seemed rather late to start raising objections. He consoled himself with the thought that the river was not dangerous at that point, and that provided they didn't fall overboard they were unlikely to come to any harm.

"It's only a suggestion, like, but if you're both going to row it might help matters if you were both facing the same way," he advised.

"Yes, of course!" Jennings agreed. "You are an ignorant bazooka, Darbishire. Surely you know you have to sit facing backwards if you want to row forwards."

"I can't face backwards. I haven't got eyes in the back of my head!" the new oarsman protested.

At last, however, they were properly seated, and for the second time the boatman pushed the craft well away from the bank.

For a while their progress was erratic and the boat veered first to port and then to starboard as each boy heaved on his oar and made no attempt to keep in time with the other.

"This is hopeless! I reckon we must be in a whirlpool or something," complained Darbishire, resting upon his oar. "We're swirling round like a soap-sud going down the bathroom waste-pipe."

"We're not dipping our oars in together – that's why,"

71

Jennings pointed out. "Pull harder and take your time from me. Ready? Heave-ho! ... In ... out ... In ... out ... In ...."

"Hey, not so much of the *heav-ho*-ing! I haven't come out after going in the first time, yet," his fellow oarsman complained. "You seem to forget I've got to go carefully to start with. If this oar jumps out before I'm ready, I shall go over backwards."

By this time the boat had circled its way out into the middle of the river where, borne along by the current, it began to drift downstream. Gradually, by trial and error, the rowers remedied the worst features of their oarsmanship and were able to keep on a fairly even course.

"That's better! Now we really *are* going!" Jennings crowed happily after some ten minutes of haphazard drifting. "Let's pretend we're in the Boat Race, shall we? I'll be Oxford and you be Cambridge."

"You can't have both crews in the same boat. They've got to row against each other."

"That's what we *have* been doing up to now," said Jennings. "All right, then. Let's pretend we're shipwrecked mariners in a lifeboat miles from anywhere, and we're trying to reach an uninhabited island."

"Wow, yes, of course! Our island! I'd almost forgotten about that," Darbishire exclaimed.

Indeed, they had both been so absorbed in the flurry and turmoil of trying to bring the boat under control that, until that moment, they had had no thought to spare for the original object of their expedition. Already they had frittered away nearly half their allotted time. There was not another second to be lost!

Jennings glanced up and down the river and his brows

met in a puzzled frown. The island was nowhere to be seen.

"That's funny. It's gone," he exclaimed.

"It must be round the bend – farther upstream," Darbishire decided. "Yes, now I come to think of it, we were on the other side of the river when we spotted it last week. We've been rowing the wrong way all the time!"

"Oh, fish-hooks! Let's turn the boat round quickly."

It was then that they found themselves beset by further troubles. The friendly current which had been carrying them downstream so smoothly now proved to be an implacable enemy when they began to row against it. After five minutes of strenuous toil they found they had made no progress whatever. Rather the reverse, for they were now a hundred yards farther down the river, and drifting slowly past a private landing stage at the end of a garden belonging to a riverside house.

"This is frantic!" moaned Darbishire. "We'll never get back to the boat-house before our half-hour is up – let alone get past it and round the bend to our island."

"And what's the boatman going to say? I haven't got any more money to pay for the overtime." Worried now, Jennings said, "Here, let's change places, Darbi. We might get on quicker if I had the left-handed oar."

"We'd better not move around now, while the boat's out of its depth. My father says you should never change horses in midstream and . . ."

"Oh, don't natter, Darbi! I'm talking about changing *places* – not changing horses," Jennings said irritably. "Although for all the use you are I'd just as soon have a horse in the boat as . . ." He broke off, struck by a sudden

73

bright idea. "Yes, of course! They use horses to tow barges along canals, don't they?"

"What's that got to do with . . .?"

"You could be the horse, Darbi, and walk along the bank towing the boat by the mooring rope."

"Well, I like the cheek of that!" grumbled Darbishire. "You invite me to come on a secret expedition; then expect me to pay fifty pence; then tell me you can't manage the boat; then tell me I've got to trudge along towing the wretched thing like a beast of burden while you sit there saying 'Gee-up' and 'Whoa'!"

"We'll never get back in time otherwise," Jennings argued. "If we pull in at that landing stage over there you can hop out and start pulling, and then we shan't be more than about ten minutes late after all."

Darbishire glanced across the water and noticed that the landing stage was no longer empty. A small, thin, elderly man in a linen jacket and panama hat was untying a skiff from its mooring post.

"It's private property over there," Darbishire demurred. "That old boy may not like us using his landing stage."

"He won't mind if we tell him it's an emergency. Come on, Darbi, pull for the shore. It's our only hope of getting the boat back without paying overtime."

They bent low over their oars and rowed with grim determination. So engrossed were they in their task that they had no eye to spare for what was going on behind them, and did not notice that the thin man in the panama hat had boarded his skiff and was now reversing it into midstream.

Their failure to keep a sharp look-out was doubly

unfortunate, for the elderly oarsman – like Jennings and Darbishire – was equally lacking in any sense of navigation. He, too, failed to keep a watchful eye on the river and seemed quite unaware of the presence of another craft.

For some moments the two boats headed straight towards each other. Nearer and nearer they came until they were only a few feet apart.

Then Jennings glanced over his shoulder. "Wow! Help! Whoa! Stop! Full speed astern!" he shouted in sudden panic.

The warning came too late. For the next second the skiff bumped heavily into the stern of the rowing boat, lurched drunkenly and then tipped over on its side, throwing its elderly occupant into the water.

The accident happened so suddenly that for a moment both boys seemed paralysed with shock. But the sight of the elderly oarsman's head rising to the surface some distance away galvanised Jennings into activity.

"Quick, Darbi! To the rescue! Row like mad!" he shouted.

Darbishire let out a wail of despair. "But I can only row *round* and *round* with one oar! It's no good rowing in circles, however madly!" he cried.

"Yes it is! Swing the boat round: then we'll be able to reach him."

From the water came gurgling appeals for help.

"Ach! gll! pff! Pull me out! I'm sinking," gasped the little man. He struck out towards the boat, but it was plain that he was a poor swimmer, and after a few clumsy strokes he sank beneath the surface only to reappear a moment later gulping for breath and lashing out unskil-

fully with his arms. Oddly enough, his panama hat had not been dislodged by the ducking and remained on his head, jammed well down over his ears.

More by luck than judgment, the boys pulled the boat across to the struggling swimmer, and Jennings leaned over the side to grasp the wildly waving hands.

"All right, I've got you. Keep still and I'll try and pull you aboard," he panted.

The rowing boat lurched dangerously.

"Look out, Jen! You'll have the boat over!" Darbishire shouted in alarm.

"But I can't reach him unless I lean out!"

"We'll capsize if you don't keep still. Then we'll all be in the river!"

By this time Jennings had seized the floundering swimmer by one hand, but every effort he made to haul him aboard caused the rowing boat to rock and sway in the most perilous manner.

"This is hopeless. We'll never get him in like this," Darbishire moaned. "I'm beginning to feel seasick already, and . . ."

Jennings made a quick decision. "We'll trail him along behind the boat," he said. "I'll hold his hands while you row us to the bank, Darbi."

In this way they eventually reached the landing stage from which the elderly oarsman had set out a few minutes before. It was not an easy journey for any of them. Darbishire was hard put to it to manage the boat: using only one oar, he propelled the craft in a series of lopsided circles, while Jennings strained to retain his balance against the pull of the little man trailing behind them in the water like some aquatic monster on the end of a fishing line.

At last, however, they reached the shallow water near the bank. Choking and spluttering, the forlorn figure in the linen jacket struggled out of the river, while the two boys scrambled from the boat and helped him on to dry land.

Chapter 7

Plan of escape

Jennings heaved a sigh of heart-felt relief. "Phew!! That was a narrow squeak!" he gasped, looking anxiously at the rescued oarsman. "Are you all right? – apart from being soaked through, of course."

It took a little while for the bedraggled figure to recover enough breath to speak. When he had done so he said, "I'm not quite sure. I haven't had time to make a thorough investigation yet." In spite of the shock to which he had been subjected, he spoke in mild, almost apologetic tones, and favoured his rescuers with a watery smile.

The boys felt better when they saw the smile, for they had been expecting him to rant with rage and to hold them solely to blame for the collision.

"I'm terribly sorry about what happened," Darbishire began. "You see, we were trying to . . ."

"Please don't apologise. My fault entirely," came the unexpected reply. "Unfortunately, I came out without my glasses or I should certainly have noticed you in time."

"It's fantastic of you to put it like that, but we were just as much to blame as you were," Jennings confessed.

The little man didn't seem to have heard him. "On second thoughts, perhaps it's as well that I *did* leave them behind, or I might have lost them when I fell into the water," he rambled on, as though talking more to himself than to his listeners. "On third thoughts, however, it occurs to me that had I been wearing them I should have seen you coming, so – so . . ."

He tailed off into silence, unable to decide whether or not his lack of spectacles had been a disadvantage. After a pause he went on, "I'm most grateful to you for coming to my rescue like that. Mind you, if the water hadn't been so cold I should have been able to struggle out by myself, but when it's as chilly as that I just curl up and can't swim."

"Stickly-Prickly, that's him," murmured Darbishire.

"I beg your pardon?"

"Oh, nothing. It's just that you reminded me of a quotation from a story we read in class: *Curls up and can't swim, Stickly-Prickly, that's him*. He's a hedgehog, you see."

The elderly gentleman looked puzzled. "And why should I remind you of a hedgehog?"

"Oh, you don't really," Darbishire hastened to explain. "He's just a character in one of Rudyard Kipling's stories."

"Just so," said the little man gravely. "And now perhaps we had better introduce ourselves, I'm most anxious to know the names of my brave rescuers."

Jennings felt distinctly uncomfortable. Surely there was no need for all this gratitude, especially as they themselves had been largely to blame for the accident. "My name's

Jennings, and this is my friend Darbishire," he said unwillingly. "We go to a boarding school a few miles from here."

"S-s-splendid!" As he spoke a convulsive shudder ran through the rescued oarsman's slender frame. Until then, the shock of his immersion had made him unmindful of his cold and damp condition, but now, with the fresh breeze chilling him to the bone, he began to shiver so violently that he was almost unable to speak.

"And m-my n-name's Hip-Hip-Hip . . ."

Jennings suppressed an impulse to shout "Hooray!"

". . . Hipkin," the little man stuttered through chattering teeth. "Doctor Ba-ba-ba . . ."

They waited patiently. There must be more to come. No one outside the nursery could have a name like *Ba-ba*.

"Dr Basil Hipkin. I live in that h-house up there. You m-must come up and m-meet my w-w-wife. She'll be de-de-de-de . . ."

"It's very kind of you, but I'm afraid we'll have to be going straight away," said Darbishire, without waiting for Dr Hipkin to finish his stammering statement. "We're late already, aren't we, Jen?"

He glanced round and noticed that his friend had left his side and was down by the water's edge trying to reach Dr Hipkin's overturned skiff, which was drifting back towards the bank. Darbishire hurried down to help, and after some difficulty they managed to secure the trailing painter at the trifling expense of getting wet through up to their knees. Then they towed the boat along to the mooring post and made it fast while the doctor stood dripping damply and stuttering vague thanks.

By now it was well after half past three, and Jennings and Darbishire were anxious to make their way back up the river without losing any more time. But as they were preparing to set off they heard the sound of approaching footsteps, and turned to see a tall, middle-aged woman striding along the path which led from the house down to the landing stage.

"This is my w-w-wife," explained Dr Hipkin. "She'll be de-de-de . . ."

"Good gracious, Basil, what's happened? You're wringing wet!" Mrs Hipkin exclaimed in vibrant tones as she hurried towards them. "You don't mean to say you've been careless enough to fall into the water?"

The doctor controlled his chattering teeth and waved a hand at Jennings and Darbishire.

"I'm afraid so, my dear. Just a slight case of accidental shipwreck, as you might say," he replied apologetically. "But everything was all right, as it happened. At great personal risk these brave boys rescued me from a w-watery grave."

"Splendid! Well done, boys. Well done!" cried Mrs Hipkin. "I always tell my husband that he's not really capable of managing the skiff by himself, but he insists upon trying. Thank goodness there were a couple of gall-ant rescuers to come to his aid at the critical moment."

The gallant rescuers exchanged sheepish glances. High praise was the last thing they had been expecting.

"Highly commendable conduct," agreed Dr Hipkin with a slight shiver. "In fact, if it hadn't been for them, Amanda, I should have been a-a-a-*achoo*!"

A loud sneeze shattered the stillness of the afternoon, and Mrs Hipkin swung round on her husband in stern rebuke. "Basil, you've caught a cold!"

"No, no, dear. Just a touch of hay fever," he hastened to explain.

"Nonsense. You must have a hot bath and go to bed at

once." Seen at close quarters, Mrs Hipkin was a woman of commanding presence who obviously possessed a forceful personality. She turned to Jennings and Darbishire. "Come along, boys. We'll go indoors and you can tell me all about it over a cup of tea."

"Oh, but, really, we must be going," Jennings demurred. "You see, we've only hired this boat for half an hour and we're late taking it back and we haven't got any more money to pay for the overtime."

"That's all right. I'll fix everything up with the boat-man," Mrs Hipkin said in tones that brooked no argument. "Besides, I can't allow the heroes of the hour to slip away before they've been properly thanked."

Her next words fell upon the ears of her youthful audience with a shock of horror and dismay. "And what's more, I intend to see that this brave deed of yours receives widespread recognition. Your headmaster will indeed be a proud man when he hears of your exploits this afternoon."

For some moments Jennings and Darbishire were too overcome to speak and stood staring at Mrs Hipkin in a trance of despair and embarrassment. Jennings was the first to find his voice.

"Oh, but *please*, you musn't tell the Head about it," he implored. "There'd be the most frantic hoo-hah – I mean the most terrible trouble – if he found out where we'd been this afternoon."

"We're not allowed on the river, you see – it's out of bounds," Darbishire explained with a gulp. "And anyway, we're supposed to be back at school watching a cricket match this afternoon."

Mrs Hipkin had scant respect for school rules. "Nonsense! Why, if you hadn't been on hand to rescue my husband, goodness knows what might have happened," she boomed. "You leave your headmaster to me. I'll soon put matters right. When I tell him that he has every reason to be proud of your brave . . ."

"*A-toosh*!" interrupted Dr Hipkin loudly. He did his best to stifle the sneeze, but merely succeeded in emitting a sound like a badly blown bugle. His wife waved an accusing forefinger in his direction.

"Don't try to tell me *that* was hay fever, Basil," she said severely. "You'll catch your death of cold standing there with your teeth chattering like that. Come along! We must stop shilly-shallying and go indoors at once. We can straighten out this nonsense about stupid school rules when we get inside."

She spoke in tones of brisk authority, and it was quite clear that she was accustomed to having her orders obeyed without question. Indeed, so forceful was her personality that Jennings and Darbishire found themselves being shepherded up the path and into the house before they had had another chance to protest against the unwelcome hospitality being forced upon them.

At the front door, Jennings conceived the notion of making a sudden dash for freedom, but on second thoughts he abandoned the idea as impractical. To begin with, Dr Hipkin already knew their names and might start inquiries to find out which school they attended. Besides, they would have to leave their address with the boatman as they had not enough ready money to pay his account. All things considered, it would be wiser to accept the Hipkins' invitation. Perhaps, over a cup of tea, their hosts could be persuaded to abandon their intentions of reporting the facts to Mr Pemberton-Oakes.

"Here we are, boys," said Mrs Hipkin, leading the way into the living-room. "Take your shoes and socks off, and I'll switch the electric fire on to dry them. Then, as soon as the doctor's had a hot bath and we've all had a cup of tea, I'll run you back to school in the car."

Jennings was quick to raise an objection to this horrifying plan. "But we've got bicycles," he pointed out. "We've left them down by the boat-house, so we shan't be able to . . ."

"That's all right. We can pop them in the back," came the devastating reply. "It's a big estate car, you see. Plenty of room for you and the bikes."

Jennings' hopes sank once more. Was there no way of convincing this well-meaning woman that her misguided meddling was going to land them in serious trouble? The mind boggled at what would happen if the headmaster were to hear that they had spent the afternoon out of bounds, breaking school rules in this flagrant fashion.

Unfortunately, Mrs Hipkin was unable to appreciate this point of view when Jennings tried to reason with her. The boys had performed a heroic deed of rescue, had they not? Very well, then! The school should be proud of them, and would certainly welcome the chance to fête its heroes in a manner fitting to the occasion.

With a wave of her hand she swept aside the boys' plea for secrecy and strode off into the kitchen to make the tea, determined that the so-called act of bravery should be accorded the publicity it so richly deserved.

As the door closed behind her, Darbishire uttered a groan of despair.

"This is ghastly! The Head will go off like a nuclear bomb when he hears what we've done."

Jennings nodded in agreement. "And it's no good trying to explain school rules to people like Mrs Hipkin. They mean well, but they just don't understand."

"Let's escape!" cried Darbishire in sudden panic. "Let's beetle out before she comes back with the tea." In frantic haste he struggled back into his wet shoes and socks which he had taken off a few minutes before.

Then, leaping to his feet, he rushed out into the hall, where a number of doors confronted him. Heedless of any sense of direction, he opened one at random . . . and found himself in the kitchen where Mrs Hipkin was brewing the tea.

"Have you come to help me?" she inquired pleasantly.

"Er – well – I . . ." Darbishire stammered, fidgeting from foot to foot in embarrassment.

"I don't think there's anything you can do at the

moment," his hostess went on. "Just make yourselves comfortable in the living-room. I shall be bringing the tray through in a moment, so you might leave the door open for me."

Baffled, Darbishire returned to the living-room to report the failure of his mission.

"What makes it a whole lot worse is that we can't even try again because she made me leave the door open," he fumed, pacing about the room and leaving a trail of wet footprints all over the carpet. "She'd be able to see us foxing across the hall if we tried to make a bolt for the front door."

"It's probably bolted already, so in any case we shouldn't be able to . . ."

"No, what I mean is . . ."

"Oh, don't natter, Darbi!" Jennings broke in peevishly. "It wouldn't help much even if we *did* escape. We'd have to go and collect our bikes first of all, and that'd mean explaining to the boatman that we'd left the dinghy down the river and hadn't got any more money to pay for the overtime."

"Mrs What's-her-name said she'd settle up with him for the boat," Darbishire pointed out.

"Yes, but only if we do what she tells us. You can't expect her to pay the boatman if we start running away," Jennings reasoned. "Our only hope is to do what she says until we've got our bikes back."

"Yes, but what happens after that?" Darbishire persisted gloomily. "In half an hour from now we'll be bowling up the drive at Linbury, all set for the Head's study, with old Mrs Thingummy thinking she's doing us a favour by . . ."

His words faltered as he caught sight of the expression on his friend's face. For Jennings had jumped to his feet, his eyes gleaming with sudden inspiration.

"I've got it, Darbi! We're saved!" he cried, smiting himself on the brow in triumph. Then, lowering his voice to a whisper he went on, "I've just had a supersonic brainwave."

"What?"

"Well, they know our names, but they don't know which school we go to, so all we've got to do is to ask her to take us to the wrong one."

Darbishire frowned in bewilderment. "Talk sense, Jen. How can there be a wrong one?"

"Don't you see! We'll pick up the bikes and stow them in the car, and then direct her to Bracebridge School instead of Linbury. She'll go off inside to find the Head, and he'll say he's never heard of us, and that'll lead to a bit of an argument."

Darbishire's eyes gleamed with excitement as the plot was unfolded. "Go on, Jen. What next?"

"Well, while she's indoors arguing with the Bracebridge headmaster, we'll get our bikes out of the car and shoot off like a couple of ballistic missiles. We'll be safely back at Linbury before Mrs Hipkin has straightened out the shemozzle."

"Oh, lobsterous scheme! Oh, fantastic wheeze!" Darbishire chortled in glee. "Honestly, Jen, you must have got a super-electronic brain unit to think out a plan like that. And the best of it is that we can't possibly be recognised at Bracebridge because there's nobody there who knows us."

They beamed at each other in satisfied triumph ... It was as well for their peace of mind that they did not know

87

that the Linbury Court 2nd XI had been batting on the Bracebridge cricket ground for the past half hour.

When Mrs Hipkin came in with the tea a few minutes later, Jennings and Darbishire raised no further objection to her offer to run them back to school in the car. Instead, they sipped their tea and left their hostess to do all the talking. She told them, amongst other things, that her husband had decided to retire to bed after his hot bath, in the hope of shaking off his threatened cold. It appeared that he was not a doctor of medicine, as they had supposed, but a doctor of science now engaged in writing a book about his work. Jennings listened with half an ear, not particularly interested in the details of the doctor's researches. In fact, it was not until very much later in the term that he found out in which branch of science Dr Hipkin specialised.

After tea Mrs Hipkin chivvied her guests into a large, shabby estate car and drove them to the boat-house. A few words from her satisfied the boatman that he need have no fears for the safety of his craft, or the money outstanding for its hire. Then they set off on the second stage of their journey.

"Come along, boys, jump in," Mrs Hipkin boomed in hearty tones, when the two bicycles had been stowed in the back of the car.

"You're sure you really *do* want to take us back?" Jennings queried. "I mean, we'd much rather go by ourselves, honestly."

"Nonsense! I wouldn't dream of it. I feel it's my duty to thank your headmaster in person, and tell him what a credit you boys are to his school."

Darbishire swallowed hard as he clambered into the

estate car. Only too well could he picture the reactions of Mr Pemberton-Oakes on hearing this surprising news.

"Now then, which way do we go?" demanded Mrs Hipkin, as she started the car.

"I think you'd better turn left at the end of this road," Jennings replied, trying hard to remember the way to Bracebridge. "Then bear right along the main road till you see a big – er – er . . ."

For the life of him he couldn't remember what the neighbouring school looked like at close quarters. This was not surprising, for it was only on rare occasions that he had been there as a member of a visiting team. Vaguely he finished up, "Well, I *think* it's a red brick building."

"No, it isn't, Jen. It's grey stone, with a slate roof," Darbishire pointed out.

"Is it? I can't remember."

Mrs Hipkin's eyebrows rose in surprise. "You're not very observant, are you?" she remarked. "Surely you know what your own school looks like."

"Well – er . . ." Jennings searched his mind for some more convincing details. "Well, anyway, go on till you get to a gate with a brass plate on it saying 'Bracebridge School.' You can't miss it when once you get to the main road."

"Bracebridge School!" Mrs Hipkin echoed as the car gathered speed. "Right! Now we shan't be long."

Chapter 8

The Plan Misfires

The Linbury Court 2nd XI had scored fifty-four runs for the loss of nine wickets when the estate car, with Mrs Hipkin at the wheel, turned in through the main gates of Bracebridge School and made its way up the drive which bordered the cricket field.

Temple and Venables were squatting on the bank with their backs to the drive watching the game with keen interest. As batsmen nos. 7 and 9, they had finished their innings and were feeling reasonably pleased with their efforts. For amongst the tail-enders of the 2nd XI, the ability to score any runs at all was looked upon as something of an achievement; and in this respect Temple and Venables had succeeded as the entries in the score-book proved. (Temple, bowled Archer – 4 . . . Venables, run out – 1.) Now they could afford to relax in the sunshine and criticise Atkinson's policy of smiting towards the square leg umpire all balls which pitched outside his off stump.

"I bet the Archbeako ticks him off for that in the tea break," Temple prophesied. "Still, he's broken his duck, so I suppose he can afford to take a few risks."

At that moment the estate car swept up the wide gravelled drive some twenty yards behind them. Venables turned his head to watch it pass and then wrinkled his nose in puzzled wonder. "Hey, did you see those two oiks in that car?" he queried. "They looked like Jennings and Darbishire to me."

Temple snorted in derision. "You're crazy! How could it be when they're not in the team?" He glanced at his watch and added, "They'll be having tea back at school, round about now."

"I didn't say it *was*. I said it *looked* like them," Venables persisted. "If you don't believe me, go and have a squint at close quarters and you'll see what I mean."

"Come on, then," Temple agreed, jumping to his feet. "But I bet you a million pounds you're wrong."

By this time the car had stopped outside the front door and the driver and her passengers were alighting at the foot of the steps.

Jennings kept his fingers crossed. So far his plan was working well. The next stage, involving a headlong dash for freedom on bicycles as soon as Mrs Hipkin had disappeared indoors, might be more difficult to achieve.

"We'll wait here, if you don't mind, Mrs Hipkin," Jennings said with what confidence he could muster. "I expect you'll find the Head somewhere about, if you go in and ask."

"Very well," she replied. "But I haven't met the headmaster before. What does he look like?"

Jennings' jaw dropped slightly. To the best of his

knowledge he had never seen the Bracebridge headmaster either. "He's – er – well, I don't really know," he faltered.

"You don't know! But you *must* know! Is he tall or short: young or old?"

"I should say he's – well, fairly tall and dark, wouldn't you, Darbishire?"

"M'yes," his friend agreed solemnly. "Though if anything, I should describe him as somewhat on the short side and going a bit bald. And quite old, of course – well, about thirty at least."

Mrs Hipkin stared at them in growing perplexity. "You really are the most unobservant boys I've ever met," she exclaimed. "First you can't remember what your school buildings look like, and now you tell me to look out for a tall, dark man who at the same time is short and bald-headed!" As she strode up the steps and in through the open front door she added, "I think I'll get on a lot faster if I make my own inquiries, thank you."

As soon as she was out of sight, Jennings and Darbishire opened the rear door of the car and lifted their bicycles down on to the drive.

"Quick, Darbi, let's get cracking. We haven't much time," Jennings urged as he prepared to mount his machine. "If she can't find the Head, she'll come beetling out again in two bats of an eyelid to ask . . ."

He stopped abruptly, and stared wide-eyed and open-mouthed at two figures in white flannels and blazers who came trotting along the drive towards him.

"Venables! . . . Temple! . . . What on earth are you doing here?" he gasped.

"That's just what I was going to ask you," Venables

replied with equal bewilderment. "It's obvious why *we* are here. We're playing in the match."

"But it's a *home* match. You ought to be back at Linbury – not at Bracebridge."

Temple tapped the side of his forehead in a pitying manner. "You're off your rocker, Jen," he said. "You must have heard Mr Carter give out the notice that we were going to come over here for the match."

"No, I didn't. We got permish to go to the village just after lunch."

"Well, anyway, it was altered because our pitch was too wet and we had to come here instead. Venables and I came over in the Head's car, and . . ."

"What! You don't mean to say the Archbeako is over here too!" Jennings cried aghast. A glance at the pavilion away to his right confirmed his worst fears. Seated comfortably in deck-chairs were the headmaster and Mr Carter, while out on the cricket pitch Mr Wilkins could be seen umpiring at the bowler's end.

"Oh, fish-hooks, this is frantic!" moaned Darbishire, as with one accord the two boys abandoned their bicycles and scuttled behind the car for shelter. "We came here specially on purpose because we thought they wouldn't be here! In fact, we almost knew for certain that they couldn't *possibly* be here. And now look!" He edged a bit farther behind the protective cover of the estate car and went on: "It would have been a whole lot more sensible if we'd asked her to take us straight back to Linbury. At least the Head wouldn't have been at home and we might have got rid of her before he came back."

Darbishire had certainly raised a point. Perhaps, even now, it would not be too late to modify the plan of escape.

With one accord they scuttled behind the car.

"All right, then. We'll try and get her to take us away before she gets a chance to talk to the Archbeako," Jennings agreed.

Venables and Temple had been listening to this conversation with uncomprehending ears.

"What's up? What's all the flap about?" Temple wanted to know.

"Yes, and why are you two characters here instead of being at home?" Venables demanded.

Jennings dismissed the queries with an impatient shrug. "Can't explain now. It's just that we did somebody a good turn, and they want to tell the Head all about it."

"Well, why not?"

"Why not!" Jennings echoed with a gulp of despair. "I'll tell you why not. Because if we hadn't been out of bounds on the river in a hired boat we couldn't even finish paying for, we shouldn't have *done* them a good turn."

"Wow! You haven't half got yourselves up a gum tree this time," Temple said with relish.

At that moment footsteps sounded close at hand and, swinging round, Jennings saw Mrs Hipkin emerging through the front door. Venables and Temple, scenting trouble, sidled away to the cricket field.

It was not often that Mrs Hipkin's genial temper became ruffled, but now she wore a slight frown of impatience. She had been informed by a housemaid that the headmaster was not in the building and that his precise whereabouts were unknown. He might be in the pavilion watching the cricket match, and then again, he might not: the housemaid couldn't say. And from the off-hand way in which she spoke it was clear that she didn't care either.

Mrs Hipkin was annoyed at the casual manner in which

her inquiry was answered. Furthermore, she was in no mood for wasting time, for she was due at the vicarage for a committee meeting later in the afternoon, and was anxious to meet the headmaster and explain the reason for her visit without delay.

But, most of all, she was perturbed by the boys' evasive answers to her questions. It was all very well for them to be modest about their courageous action on the river. Such humility was all to their credit. But there was more to it than that, she felt certain. Surely there was no reason for them to be vague about straightforward matters such as a description of their school, or the appearance of their headmaster! She would stand no more of these evasive answers, she decided. She would get to the root of the matter right away. With this intention she swept out of the building and marched down the steps. . . . But when she reached her car a further shock awaited her.

"Excuse me, Mrs Hipkin," Jennings began apologetically. "I'm awfully sorry, but there's been a bit of a bish . . . *We've come to the wrong school!*"

Mrs Hipkin rocked on her heels in astonishment. "We've done *what!*"

"It's rather difficult to explain, you see, only . . ."

"But, good heavens, boy, surely you know which school you go to!"

"Oh yes, of course, but you see . . ."

"Then stop talking such arrant nonsense! I'm in a hurry and I want to see your headmaster immediately." Her gaze swept across the cricket field and came to rest upon Mr Pemberton-Oakes seated in a deck-chair beside the pavilion. "Now, who is that man over there?" she demanded.

Darbishire shuffled uncomfortably. "Well, actually, that *is* the headmaster, but . . ."

"Then why on earth didn't you say so before, instead of letting me waste my time traipsing round the building looking for him!" With a frown of reproof, Mrs Hipkin turned and strode vigorously off towards the pavilion, leaving Jennings and Darbishire staring after her in horror and dismay.

Although the standard of play was not high, Mr Pemberton-Oakes was enjoying the match as he reclined in his deck-chair in the warm rays of the afternoon sun. From time to time he would close his eyes in anguish to blot out the sight of some wildly unorthodox stroke. But this was a mere gesture of protest and did not detract from the pleasure he felt at the team's obvious enthusiasm.

More by luck than judgment, Atkinson and his partner were still batting in a dogged last wicket stand. They had made five runs between them in the previous quarter of an hour, during which time the total score had crept up by thirteen runs owing to the frequency of the wides and byes given away by the fielding side. At the present rate of progress there seemed a slight chance that the erratic bowling of the Bracebridge team would enable their opponents to score a century before the last wicket fell.

With this hope in mind, Mr Pemberton-Oakes was following the progress of the game, ball by ball. He was, therefore, vaguely annoyed when a large lady with a forceful personality came striding up to him and distracted his attention from the match.

"Good afternoon. My name is Hipkin," she announced in ringing tones. "I don't think we've met, though you may have heard of my husband, Dr Hipkin. His name is often mentioned in scientific and scholastic circles."

"Oh – ah – yes, of course. To be sure," Mr Pemberton-Oakes murmured, as he rose to his feet wondering who on earth Dr Hipkin was, and what his claim to fame might be.

"I understand you're the headmaster," Mrs Hipkin went on, "and that being so, I should like to congratulate you upon the courageous and gallant conduct of two of your boys."

Mr Pemberton-Oakes held up a restraining hand. "One moment, please. I am *not* the headmaster of Bracebridge School."

"You're not! But the boys just told me you were!" A flicker of exasperation passed across Mrs Hipkin's features. "This is ridiculous! First they don't know which school they go to, and now they don't recognise their own headmaster when they see him."

"I think I see how the misunderstanding arose," Mr Pemberton-Oakes hastened to explain. "I am *a* headmaster, but not *the* headmaster, if you follow me."

From the expression on her face it was clear that Mrs Hipkin did *not* follow. Just how many headmasters were there in this school, she wondered?

"I am the headmaster of Linbury Court – a neighbouring school," Mr Pemberton-Oakes went on. "I've brought my boys over here for a cricket match. The man you want to see is Mr Parkinson, the head of Bracebridge. Unfortunately he's had to go out, but he told me he hopes to be back before stumps are drawn at half past six."

This news did little to reassure Mrs Hipkin. Already she was late for her committee meeting at the vicarage, and could not afford to lose more time waiting for the return of the appropriate headmaster. The only thing to be done was to explain the reason for her visit to Mr Pemberton-Oakes, and ask him to pass on the information to Mr

Parkinson when he returned. Accordingly, she embarked upon a stirring account of the rescue on the river and the gallantry of the two schoolboys who had come to the aid of her husband.

"And I think some recognition of this noble act is called for," she finished up. Favouring Mr Pemberton-Oakes with a winning smile, she said: "I'm quite sure that if they had been boys from *your* school, instead of Bracebridge, you would reward them with – er – well, with a half holiday, or something of the sort."

Mr Pemberton-Oakes stroked his chin and pursed his lips thoughtfully. "Well, *my* boys are not allowed on the river, so the circumstances could not possibly arise," he answered. "But were I the headmaster of a school where unsupervised rowing formed part of the curriculum – as apparently it does here at Bracebridge – then I should be inclined to agree that a half holiday would be a fitting reward for such valiant conduct."

"Exactly," approved Mrs Hipkin. "And I shall be more than grateful if you will recount the circumstances to the headmaster of Bracebridge upon his return – not forgetting the half holiday, of course." Whereupon she shook hands with Mr Pemberton-Oakes, smiled affably at Mr Carter, and strode back towards the drive.

When she had gone a few steps, the headmaster was struck by a sudden thought.

"One moment, Mrs Hipkin," he called. "You didn't mention the names of the boys concerned. Mr Parkinson will certainly want to know who they are."

"Yes, of course. How stupid of me." Mrs Hipkin paused in her stride and wrinkled her brow in thought. "Let me see, now. Ah, yes! One of them was called Jennings, and the other one Darbishire. Well, I really must be off. Goodbye!"

So saying, she crunched heavily up the gravel drive, leaving Mr Pemberton-Oakes gaping after her in dumb-founded astonishment. By the time he had recovered the power of speech and action, the estate car was gathering speed on its way to the main gate.

"Jennings and Darbishire – it *would* be," the head-master murmured faintly. He turned to Mr Carter who had been standing close by and listening to Mrs Hipkin's recital with keen interest.

"Jennings and Darbishire. That *was* what she said, wasn't it, Carter?"

His assistant nodded. "I don't know why she thought they belonged to Bracebridge, but it certainly seems as though they've been out on the river without permission."

"Exactly! And as soon as I return home I shall send for them and – and . . ."

The headmaster's voice died away in a further shock of surprise. For there, in the distance, vainly trying to conceal themselves behind an inadequate poplar tree, were the two boys in question. . . . It was fantastic! How on earth did they come to be here in Bracebridge when, by rights, they should be eating their tea in the dining hall at Lin-bury Court, seven miles away?

Mr Carter had seen the fugitives by this time. He waved to attract their attention and crooked a finger to indicate that their presence was requested.

As they awaited the boys' approach, the headmaster frowned and tightened his lips grimly. "This is extremely serious: I shall have to punish them severely," he observed.

"Quite so! And after that?" Mr Carter inquired.

"After that? I don't follow you."

"After you've punished them, are you going to grant the half holiday which you agreed with Mrs Hipkin was a fitting reward for their conduct?"

"I – I – Oh, but surely ..." Mr Pemberton-Oakes glanced sharply at his assistant and then looked away again, conscious that Mr Carter had raised a somewhat thorny problem. True, the headmaster had agreed that the gallant rescue should be properly rewarded: but that was when he was under the impression that his own boys were not involved. Now that he knew the identity of the rescuers he was not so certain. He was roused from his reflections by the arrival of Jennings and Darbishire, who stood before him in guilty silence.

"Well?" demanded the headmaster in ominous tones.

Jennings swallowed hard. "Please, sir, we're very sorry we pulled Dr Hipkin out of the river, sir."

"Sorry!"

"Well, no, not really, sir. I mean, we're glad we rescued him, but we're sorry we – er – well, what I mean is ..."

The faltering apology rambled on, and after some minutes of confused explanation the headmaster managed to piece together an account of the afternoon's activities. When he had heard all the facts he pondered for some while before speaking. Normally there would be no doubt as to what would happen next – punishment would follow crime. But this time the circumstances were rather unusual.

Finally the headmaster said, "Your conduct this afternoon, Jennings and Darbishire, has placed me in a difficult position. On the one hand you deserve to be severely punished for breaking school rules ..."

"Yes, sir, I know, sir," Jennings concurred humbly.

". . . on the other hand, I am filled with admiration for your prompt action in a sudden emergency, and as Mr Carter insists on reminding me, I agreed that such behaviour might well merit a half holiday for the school. Frankly, I am at a loss to know how to decide between these opposing points of view."

There was a short silence. Then Jennings said, "Well, sir, I know what you *could* do."

"Carry on, Jennings. I am listening."

"You could do both, sir. The half holiday and the punishment at the same time, sir."

The headmaster looked puzzled. "And what exactly do you mean by that profound remark?"

"Well, sir, you could give out that there was going to be a half holiday for the whole school, sir, and then, just as it was going to start, you could put Darbishire and me in detention, sir. So we'd get the punishment because we deserve it, but everybody else would be really grateful to us for getting them a half holiday, sir."

Mr Pemberton-Oakes winced and drew in his breath sharply. He had never heard such an incredible suggestion in his life. It was unthinkable! The idea of rewarding the school because two of its members had broken the rules was not one which appealed to the adult way of thinking, however logical it may have seemed to the mind of J. C. T. Jennings.

With a sigh of exasperation the headmaster turned to his assistant and said, "I think it's high time I gave all the boys a talk on the subject of school rules, Carter. You might remind me to do so one day next week. These things have a habit of slipping my memory."

"Very well, HM," Mr Carter agreed. "And what about this punishment for Jennings and Darbishire? Do you want me to remind you of that, too?"

For a moment Mr Pemberton-Oakes seemed lost in thought. Then his glance came to rest upon the two unhappy figures standing before him. From what he could gather, their ill-fated expedition had caused them so much worry and anxiety that they had already suffered as much as they deserved ... And then, if there was to be no reward, wasn't it only fair that there should be no punishment, either?

"Well, perhaps not, Carter, perhaps not," he said in more kindly tones. "If nobody reminds me about the detention, there's just a chance that *that* might slip my memory, too."

Chapter 9

Blot on the Copy Book

For the rest of the afternoon Jennings and Darbishire were allowed to watch the match. Shortly after Mrs Hipkin's departure, Atkinson absent-mindedly sat down on his wicket, while attempting to block one of the few straight balls he had received, and the Linbury innings closed for 72 runs. Then came the tea break: after which the visiting side took the field, grimly determined to give their opponents no chance of overtaking their score.

It was after the fall of the fifth wicket (Archer, bowled Temple – 4), when the score had reached the middle forties, that Jennings was smitten by a sudden pang of conscience.

"You know, Darbi, we shouldn't have gone on the river. It wasn't worth the hoo-hah," he observed in contrite tones.

Darbishire glanced up from his task of trying to persuade a hurrying beetle to climb the slippery surface of his shoe instead of making a long detour round it.

"Huh! It's a bit late in the day to start saying that now," he snorted in disgust. "You and your famous expedition! The whole thing was an absolute washout from a nature point of view. Why, we never even *saw* that island we were going to explore."

It was not often that C. E. J. Darbishire expressed himself in outspoken terms. Now, however, he felt that some curt comment was called for. After all, he had had a very nerve-racking afternoon.

"Honestly, Jen, I reckon you win the booby prize for shrimp-witted ideas against all-comers. The next time you get one of your bat-brained schemes you can flipping well leave me out of it."

Somewhat to his surprise Jennings made no attempt to justify himself. "There won't be any 'next time,' " he mumbled. "I've finished with foxing out of bounds without permish. I'm going to turn over a new leaf."

Darbishire's eyebrows shot up in surprise, and his spectacles slithered halfway down his nose. "You're going to do *what!*" he cried in disbelief.

"You heard!"

"Yes, I know, only I wasn't quite sure whether I'd got my ears tuned in to the right wavelength."

A feeling of relief swept over Darbishire. As Jennings' right-hand man he had so often, in the past, found himself facing situations from which his cautious nature recoiled in alarm. But if his friend meant what he said, there would be no cause to worry in the future. If . . .! Darbishire righted his spectacles and frowned thoughtfully. So much depended upon the *if*!

"It'll be a bit of a shock for Old Wilkie and people," he went on. "How are you going to set about it?"

Jennings pondered the matter while the fielders changed over for a left-handed batsman. "Well, for a kick-off, I'm going to work a whole lot harder in class," he resolved. "Old Wilkie's been creating quite a lot lately about my history essays and things, and it'll help to put him in a good mood."

At that moment the left-handed batsman offered a difficult catch to Venables at cover point, who greatly to his own surprise, managed to hold it. Encouraged by this feat, the Linbury bowlers pressed home their attack: wickets fell cheaply during the next half hour, and in spite of a determined stand by the Bracebridge captain, the whole side was dismissed for a total of 63 runs.

The Linbury team were jubilant about their victory as they came into the pavilion; and they were still beaming with joy as they climbed into the masters' cars for the return journey.

"There's no room for you two," Atkinson informed Jennings and Darbishire. "Old Wilkie's car's just about bursting at the seams already, so if you think you're coming in too, you're going to be unlucky."

"Who d'you think *you* are!" Jennings retorted. "After all, Atki, you're only in the team because of my blister."

"Anyway, we don't want a lift – we've got our bikes," Darbishire pointed out.

Mr Carter paused in the act of packing a cricket bag into the boot of his car. "You will *not* be cycling home, either of you," he said firmly. "After your recent exploits awheel the headmaster has arranged for your machines to be brought back by the caretaker on Monday."

"And what about us, sir?" Darbishire inquired.

"You'll have to squeeze into Mr Wilkins' car somehow

or other," Mr Carter replied. "Move up there, Atkinson, and let them get in beside you."

"Coo! Mouldy chizz!" Atkinson grumbled beneath his breath. "Fancy having to share the same car as weedy spectators!"

During the next few days, while the spirit of resolution was still strong within him, Jennings went about in a daze of virtue. Not only did he do his best in class, but he also extended his good works to include out-of-school activities ... He combed his hair (or, at least, the front part of it) before meals. He rushed to open the door whenever a master was about to leave the room. He laughed heartily at Mr Wilkins' well-worn jokes; and on two occasions he cleaned out the tadpole aquarium when it was not his turn for this tedious duty.

On Monday the bicycles arrived back from Brace-bridge, and that evening Jennings wrote and ordered one of the combination padlocks which Darbishire had seen advertised in a magazine. The letter required careful phrasing and took him some time to write.

Dear Sir, it said,
   I hope you are well and having nice weather. Please send me your guaranteed reliable combination padlock for my bicycle. I am putting in a postal order for one pound post free. It is made out with Martin-Jones' name on it as he had it in a letter from his uncle, but it is all right because I have paid him for it out of my own pocket money.
                          Yours truly,
                                  (Signed) J. C. T. Jennings.

On Wednesday afternoon there was the usual half holiday, and by common consent the members of the Form Three Natural History Club decided to employ their free time in searching the far end of the school grounds for specimens to add to their collections.

Tadpoles were in short supply: most of the batch which Jennings had caught earlier in the term had by now grown into frogs and had been taken down to the edge of the pond and set free. This was in accordance with the club rules, for it was held that whereas a tankful of tadpoles could not get up to mischief, the same could not be said for a boxful of frogs. It was all a question of security: the untimely escape of a few lively specimens would bring the club into sharp conflict with the master on duty.

Thus it was that Darbishire and, indeed, most of his fellow-naturalists, were looking forward to an afternoon spent in replenishing their dwindling stock of amphibia.

Not so Jennings!

"You go without me. I'm going to stay in and copy out my history notes into my new exercise book," he proclaimed virtuously.

The announcement was received with squawks of disbelief by the little group all ready to set out on their expedition.

"Wow! You must be stark raving crackers!" Temple gasped, sagging at the knees in exaggerated amazement. "I've met some gibbering lunatics in my time, but never anyone crazy enough to stay in on a half holiday when he didn't have to."

"Just take no notice and leave him alone," Darbishire advised. "He's turning over a new leaf, you see, and it hasn't worn off yet. It probably will in time."

"Huh! I know what it is. He's trying to get in Old Wilkie's good books," taunted Venables.

"I doubt if Old Wilkie's *got* any good books," Darbishire replied gravely. "He lent me one the other day when I'd got nothing to read, and I could hardly struggle through the first chapter."

"Come on, don't let's hang about wasting time over Jennings. We've got a job to do," said Temple. "If he wants to behave like a bat-witted imbecile that's his fault, and I hope it keeps fine for him." So saying, he scampered off towards the playing-fields with his colleagues following hard behind.

Jennings watched them go with what he hoped was a sad, wistful smile. There were more things in life than having a good time, he told himself in a glow of self-righteousness. Tadpoles weren't everything: history notes were just as important. He rather fancied the sad, wistful smile so he wore it all the way upstairs to his classroom. Outside the door he met Mr Wilkins, who glanced at him sharply and said, "Are you feeling all right, Jennings?"

"Yes, thank you, sir. Why?"

"You don't look it. What are you making that horrible face for?"

Jennings switched off the sad smile and walked into the room with what dignity he could muster.

For half an hour he sat, wrapped in a cocoon of virtue, copying into his new history book a list headed, *Important Dates in English History*. Mr Wilkins was certain to be pleased with the result, especially when he found out that the work had been done in his pupil's spare time. In his mind's eye, Jennings could visualise the scene in the classroom when the time came for the master

109

to comment upon the work of the form.

"I'm glad to see there's *one* boy who takes a real pride in his work," he would say in his loud-hailer of a voice. "Take Jennings, for instance: having filled up his old exercise-book he carefully copies the most important part . . ." With his mind concentrated on his day-dream rather than on his work, Jennings went on automatically copying out *Important Dates in English History*.

Then came the catastrophe! . . . He had just reached the entry, *Spanish Armada, 1588*, when the point of his nib speared a fragment of sodden blotting paper at the bottom of the ink-well. Unseeing and unaware, he poised the pen to write the next word . . . Too late he saw the inky pellet drop from his nib and land in a blue-black blot in the middle of the page.

He caught his breath in horror and seized the offending morsel with his fingers, smearing the tell-tale smudge over a larger area. At the same moment his pen, released from his grasp, rolled down the page, leaving an inky trail in its wake.

"Oh, fish-hooks!" he cried aloud, searching furiously for blotting paper. Unfortunately there was none to hand, and he was forced to mop up the mess with his handkerchief. Ruefully he shook his head over the ruined page which only a few moments before had contained such a splendid example of his best writing.

Something would have to be done! Perhaps he could rub out the blots and smears before the ink became too dry . . . Again the hand of fate was against him. He had no india-rubber, and could not find one in any of the neighbouring desks which he rummaged through with mounting anxiety.

Surely there must be a rubber *somewhere!*

"A fine sort of school this is, if it can't even provide a bit of bungee!" he thought bitterly.

And then he had an inspiration... Rubber bicycle pedals!

Seizing his book, he rushed from the room. Thirty seconds later he was kneeling beside his machine in the bicycle shed, massaging the page of his exercise-book with the near-side pedal.

The result was disastrous. Where previously there had been untidy inkstains, there was now, in addition, a large, dirty smear disfiguring the page wherever the pedal had touched.

Jennings groaned in dismay. His notes were ruined, the work of the afternoon completely wasted. His warm glow of virtue had congealed into an icicle of despair. For the time being, at any rate, he felt too down-hearted to continue his self-appointed task. Returning to his classroom, he hurled the book into his desk, and then wandered off to join his fellows in hunting for tadpoles behind the pond.

Darbishire was delighted to see his friend again so soon. "Finished your work?" he inquired.

Jennings shrugged. "No, not really. I made a bit of a bish. I'll have to do it again before Sir takes the books in on Friday."

"Well, anyway, you're just in time to get your jamjar ready for the big catch. Atkinson has spotted a vast shoal of tadpoles proceeding nor'-nor'-east across the pond at two knots."

The haul of tadpoles was certainly a good one, and the task of settling the specimens in their new home in the aquarium and attending to their needs occupied most of the Chief Frog Spotter's free time during the next few days.

So much so, that he forgot all about his resolve to re-copy the spoilt list of important dates until the very moment that Mr Wilkins demanded Form Three's history books on Friday afternoon. By then it was too late to put matters right, and Jennings could do nothing but keep his fingers crossed and hope for the best.

Form Three had no history lesson on Saturdays, but it was Mr Wilkins' custom to inspect the books on Friday evenings and give them back after lunch on the following day. In this way he could punish any boy whose work was not up to standard by entering his name for a detention class on Saturday afternoon.

There was no match arranged for that Saturday. Instead

"village leave" was granted, which meant that those boys who wished could go into Linbury, provided they obtained permission from the master on duty.

"How about us two going together on our bikes?" Jennings suggested to Darbishire as they came out of the dining hall after lunch. "We could call in at old Mrs Lumley's café and do a spot of refuelling on fizzy drinks and stuff."

Darbishire's eyes glistened behind his spectacles. "Great idea, Jen!" he approved.

"I was hoping my padlock would have come by today, but there's no sign of it," Jennings went on, turning in through the door of Form Three classroom. "Still, I'll just have to risk leaving it unlocked, and hope it comes on Monday."

It might have been wiser for Jennings to have awaited the return of the corrected exercise-books before making arrangements for the afternoon. For his plans were thwarted a few minutes later when Venables came into the classroom bearing a stack of history note-books.

"Old Wilkie told me to give these out. He says you're to look through them and see if he's written any comments before you ask for village leave," he announced as he handed the books back to their owners.

With a slight pang of misgiving, Jennings flicked open the cover. Then he uttered an indignant wail of protest.

"Oh, fish-hooks! Mouldy chizz! Look what he's done, Darbi!"

It would be understating the facts to say that Mr Wilkins had written comments on Jennings' book. He had, in fact, crossed out the whole of the offending page, encircling each blot and smear with an angry circle of red ink. In the margin were such remarks as *Appalling Work! Disgraceful untidiness!* and at the foot of the page was written: *Stay in and re-copy on Saturday afternoon.*

"Oh, fish-hooks! That puts the tin lid on our going into Linbury," Darbishire grumbled.

"But it's so perishing unfair," Jennings complained. "I did this work in my own free time, specially to please him. If I'd gone out and enjoyed myself, like you other oiks, I shouldn't have to stay in now. Persecution, that's what it is! Really mouldy chizz!"

"Bad luck," Temple sympathised. "Still, it's your own fault. I knew no good would come of working on a half holiday."

Jennings puffed out his cheeks in aggrieved protest and made no reply. He was aware that the spoilt pages would have to be re-copied at some later date, and indeed he had no intention of shirking this obligation. But he felt strongly that he should be allowed to do it when he chose, considering that it was a voluntary task carried out in his spare time. What seemed grossly unfair to him was the fact that he should be treated as a delinquent for attempting work which he need never have done in the first place.

Flushed with indignation, he hurried out of the classroom and along the corridor to Mr Wilkins' study. Surely, when the full facts of the matter had been explained, even Old Wilkie would be forced to admit that a grave miscarriage of justice had occurred!

Venables shook his head as Jennings disappeared through the door. "He must be crazy if he thinks Sir's going to let him off!" he observed. "Far more likely he'll get in a bate, and perhaps even double his punishment on top."

"Well, that's *his* bad luck," said Temple unfeelingly. "Come on, Ven, let's get permish to go down to the village on our bikes. I'll go and give our names in to Mr Carter."

"Righto. Meet you outside, then," Venables agreed.

But when the two boys reached the bicycle shed a few minutes later, they found to their annoyance that the back tyre of Venables' machine was punctured. Their efforts to pump it up were unsuccessful, and Venables was faced with the irksome task of removing the inner tube and repairing the damage with sticky patches and rubber solution.

Temple tut-tutted with impatience.

"I'm not going to hang about all day waiting for you to mend punctures. Can't you borrow someone else's bike just for this afternoon?" he demanded.

Venables' glance strayed round the shed and came to rest on a bright blue bicycle with white mud-guards and a union jack on the lamp bracket, parked just inside the door. There was no mistaking the ownership of *that* particular machine!

"Well, Jennings won't be using his bike if he's got to stay in and work for Old Wilkie," he reasoned. "I wonder if he'd let me borrow it."

"Of course he would," Temple replied airily. "In any case, you haven't got time to go and find him now. Just take it and ask his permish when we come back at teatime."

Venables nodded. Old Jen wouldn't mind, he decided, as he wheeled the borrowed machine from the shed and pedalled off across the playground.

Chapter 10

Daylight Robbery

Jennings' expression was serious as he faced Mr Wilkins across the study table.

"I don't like having to come to you to complain about anyone, sir, but something's happened that I don't think is fair," he began.

Mr Wilkins nodded sympathetically. If the boy was being badly treated by any of his fellows, he would do all he could to put the matter right.

"Carry on, Jennings. I'm listening."

Jennings hesitated. "Well, sir, I'm in rather an awkward pre*cad*ament, sir."

"Predicament," the master corrected.

"Yes, sir. You see, it means naming someone by name, sir, and . . ."

"Just a moment, Jennings," Mr Wilkins interrupted. "I'm willing to listen to a genuine complaint, but I don't like the idea of telling tales behind anyone's back. So I'd rather not hear what you have to say until the person you're accusing is present to defend himself."

"But the other person *is* present, sir," Jennings insisted.

Mr Wilkins looked puzzled. "I don't understand."

Taking his courage in both hands, Jennings blurted out, "You see, the other person is *you*, sir."

"Me! Good heavens! Well, why didn't you say so at once."

"I was – well, I was trying to be tactful, sir."

Mr Wilkins sighed. He could never quite understand the peculiar reasonings of the growing mind. "Well, go on then. Let's hear the worst. What am I supposed to have done?"

When he had heard the full facts of the matter Mr Wilkins relented to some extent. He could not excuse the disgraceful untidiness of the history note-book, but, all the same, it came as a shock to him to hear that Jennings had given up his half holiday in the cause of knowledge. Such industry was to be encouraged for all it was worth.

"I see. And if you'd gone off and enjoyed yourself like everybody else you wouldn't have to stay in this afternoon: is that what you mean?"

"Yes, sir."

"H'm. Well, I agree it seems a little hard to be punished for working in your own time," Mr Wilkins observed. "All right then, Jennings. You can re-copy those notes some time during the weekend, and go out this afternoon, if that's what you want."

"Thank you, sir. I hoped you'd understand."

Jennings hurried from the room, delighted that he could, after all, proceed with the afternoon's programme as planned. First he went to the staff-room where Mr

Carter was on duty, and reported that he and Darbishire proposed cycling into the village without delay.

The master on duty added their names to his list. "And you can report back to me at four o'clock sharp," he said. "After what happened last time you two went out on your bicycles, I'm going to keep a careful check on your movements."

"Yes, sir. We'll be back by four o'clock, honestly, sir."

Mr Carter turned towards a shelf beside the fireplace. "By the way, Jennings, there's a small parcel for you here," he said. "It came by the second post."

"Oh, goodo, sir. It's something I wrote up for, sir. I was hoping it would come today – it's just in time to be useful."

Excitedly he tore off the wrappings. Inside was a small cardboard box containing the combination padlock. Jennings' eyes sparkled as he turned it over and over, examining the mechanism with keen interest.

"This'll be just the job for my bike, sir," he exclaimed. "And I shan't have to bother about losing the key because this sort of padlock doesn't have one."

"Really!" said Mr Carter with mild interest.

"No, sir. It's got four rows of numbers instead, and you have to twiddle them round and get them in a certain order or the padlock won't open. Would you like to try, sir? Just say the first numbers you can think of."

Politely, Mr Carter agreed. He selected various numbers at random, though it was obvious that without knowing the combination his efforts would be in vain.

Jennings watched him with a satisfied grin of triumph.

"I'll show you the right numbers now, shall I, sir?" he said after a while. "I don't mind *your* knowing, because I know you won't go round telling everyone." He picked up the padlock and consulted the combination of figures printed on the lid of the cardboard box. "Look, sir. One – five – eight – eight." He turned the numbers round until the appropriate digits were ranged in line. There came a little click and the padlock flew open.

"There, sir! Really great, isn't it! Of course, I mustn't forget the magic numbers, or I *should* be up a gum tree, shouldn't I, sir?"

Mr Carter smiled. "If you know any English history, you should remember that number quite easily," he said.

"Why, sir?"

"It's too simple for words! One – five – eight – eight is 1588, the date of the Spanish Armada."

"Wow! Yes, of course! So it is!" Jennings was delighted with this novel method of remembering vital data. And what made it seem even more apt was the fact that it was the date of the Spanish Armada which he had been copying when he had made the fatal blot on his exercise-book.

A thought struck him and he said, "These bicycle padlocks are really useful for teaching people history, aren't they, sir? I mean, if we all had a lot of padlocks which opened at different dates, we shouldn't need history books any more, should we, sir?"

Mr Carter looked doubtful. "I *can* think of simpler ways of imparting a knowledge of the subject," he observed.

Jennings was about to leave the room when Mr Carter called him back.

"Don't you want to take the box with you?" he asked.

"No thank you, sir," Jennings replied. "I shan't forget the combination." As he hurried through the door and ran down the passage in search of Darbishire he kept repeating over and over again, "1588, the date of the Spanish Armada . . . Spanish Armada, 1588."

Darbishire was awaiting his friend at the foot of the stairs.

"It's all right, Darbi. Old Wilkie says I can go after all," Jennings greeted him. "And that supersonic combination padlock I wrote for has come, so I suggest we bike down to the village and lock the bikes up while we nip into Mrs Lumley's for those fizzy drinks and things I promised you."

Darbishire snorted in disgust. "It's no good, Jen. We can't go now. It's too late."

"No it isn't. It's only half past two, and we've got till four o'clock."

"I mean the padlock's come too late to lock the bike up. The bird has flown."

"What bird?"

"Oh, there isn't a bird, really," Darbishire replied solemnly. "It's just a saying like, for instance, locking the stable door after the horse has bolted."

Jennings eyed his friend in growing bewilderment. "What on earth are you woffling about, Darbi? I've no intention of locking up birds and horses – this padlock's for my bike."

"That's just it," Darbishire explained. "What I mean is, it's too late to talk about locking your bike up, because Venables has borrowed it to go down to the village on."

"What!" Jennings was horrified at this act of pillage.

"Yes. I saw him cycling across the playground with Temple."

"Why didn't you stop him, then?"

"I tried to, but he wouldn't. He said it'd be all right,

because you wouldn't be needing your bike as you were in detench for Old Wilkie."

"Well, I like the cheek of that!" Jennings fumed. "Just wait till I see Venables! Why, I need my bike more than ever now. What's the good of having a bicycle padlock if blokes calmly waltz off with the very thing you're supposed to use it on!"

After some discussion they agreed that Darbishire should cycle into Linbury while Jennings trotted beside him. As the village was small and boasted only three shops in its main street, they would have no trouble in finding Venables and reclaiming the machine when once they reached their destination.

"I shall have to buy a chain to put round the spokes before I can use ye famous padlock," Jennings observed as they prepared to set off on their journey. "I wonder if I could get one in the village."

"I don't see why not," Darbishire replied. "What about that shop that calls itself a Jeweller and Silversmith."

"Hey, no, I don't want a *silver* one. Any old brass chain will do, so long as it's strong enough."

"I should try the Linbury stores, then – that's the biggest place."

Jennings looked doubtful. "Yes, but they've never got anything fabulous there. What I really want is one of those multiple shops with branches all over the place."

"You mean a chain store."

"Yes, that's right. After all, if you can't buy a chain at a chain store, where *can* you get one?"

"I don't think you've quite got the idea, Jen. What I meant was . . ."

"Oh, don't natter, Darbi," Jennings broke in

impatiently. "Let's get going. I've got an urgent job to do when I get to the village – thanks to Venables."

"Yes, of course." Darbishire swung his leg over the saddle and pedalled along towards the school gates with Jennings running beside him.

It was not much more than half a mile to the village, but that was quite far enough for Jennings. As he panted along beside his comfortably mounted friend, his thoughts were steeped in vengeance.

"Just you wait till I see Venables!" he muttered. "Just you wait, that's all!"

The visitor seeking refreshment in the village of Linbury is not embarrassed by having to choose between a large number of catering establishments. The only café consists of the front parlour of a cottage at one end of the High Street, where a notice-board in the garden announces: *Chas. Lumley – Home Made Teas and Bicycles Repaired.* As a purveyor of light snacks, Mrs Lumley enjoyed a certain reputation among the boys of Linbury Court who were not slow to appreciate the quality of her home-made cakes and doughnuts, and to pass favourable comment on the fizziness of her home-made lemonade. The café was an obvious port of call whenever village leave was granted, and it was here that Jennings was hoping to find the miscreant who had so calmly gone off with his property.

Nor was he disappointed; for almost the first thing that he saw, as he panted into the High Street, was his bicycle leaning against Mrs Lumley's garden gate. Next to it was Temple's machine, which seemed to indicate that he and Venables were inside the cottage sampling the bill of fare.

"Look, Darbi – *proof*!" Jennnings cried in tones of indignation.

"Disgraceful! It makes your blood boil," his friend agreed.

"Mine's boiling already from chasing along trying to keep up with your bike," the runner complained. "Still, we've caught Venables red-handed in the act. I shan't half give him a telling off about this."

His first impulse was to march boldly into the café and give the culprit a piece of his mind. But on second thoughts he decided that this could perhaps wait until a more convenient moment. Now that he had his padlock he was most anxious to buy a chain to accompany it, for after what had happened he felt worried about leaving his machine unprotected a moment longer than necessary.

"I think I'll go and buy the chain first," he decided. "That bike isn't safe out in the street with people like Venables about."

So saying, he mounted his machine and began pedalling towards the Linbury Stores and Post Office at the far end of the village street.

"But what about Venables?" Darbishire queried as he rode along beside him.

"Well, *what* about him? He won't run away. He'll be safe enough gorging himself on doughnuts till I get back and give him a piece of my mind."

"I didn't mean that," said Darbishire. "I meant how's he going to get back to school?"

Jennings snorted loudly. "Huh! Don't you waste your sympathy on him. He can perishing well hoof all the way back on foot. After all, Darbi, that's what I had to do to get here, thanks to him. And as soon as I've got my bike safely under lock and key I shall march into Lumley's café and flipping well wipe the floor with him – you see if I don't!"

Outside the village stores they dismounted and pressed their noses against the window. There were no chains displayed on view, but doubtless they would find what they were seeking when they went inside.

"You haven't shown me your famous padlock yet," Darbishire reminded his friend as they entered the shop and made towards the counter.

"So I haven't." Jennings produced his proud possession with a flourish. "Here you are, look. It's locked at the moment and you can't open it unless you know the combination."

"And what's that?"

Jennings grinned. "I shan't tell you. Try and guess. The number's the same as the date of a famous battle."

Darbishire wrinkled his nose in thought "1066?" he hazarded.

"Wrong! I'll give you a clue. Forget the Battle of Hastings and try the Spanish Armada."

"Oh, that'd be – er – um . . ." Darbishire searched his mind in vain. Historical dates were not his strong point. "I should say somewhere in the region of fourteen? . . . fifteen? . . ."

"You're miles out," said Jennings scathingly. "1415 was the Battle of Agincourt. I know that because it was one of the dates I copied out for Sir."

"No, I meant either fourteen or fifteen hundred and something or other. Like, say, for instance . . ." He gave it up after a short mental struggle and muttered, "Well, so long as *you* know when the Armada was, that's all that matters, isn't it?"

124

But Jennings wasn't listening. He had spotted some thin metal chains dangling from a hook in what might loosely be described as the ironmongery department, and was already deep in conversation with the assistant behind the counter.

At the same time that Jennings was making his vital purchase in the Linbury Stores, Venables and Temple were finishing their fizzy drinks in Mrs Lumley's café. Soon afterwards, they paid the bill and wandered out into the village street to begin their homeward journey.

Then came the shock . . . The borrowed bicycle had disappeared.

"Crystallised cheese-cakes! What's happened!" Venables gasped in dismay. "I left it propped up against the gate next to yours!"

"Well, mine's still here," Temple pointed out. "Perhaps you left it somewhere else."

"Of course I didn't leave it somewhere else!" A quick glance up and down the street proved that the bicycle was nowhere in sight, and the dreaded conclusion flashed through Venables' mind like a streak of lightning.

"It's been stolen, that's what's happened!" he squawked.

"Stolen! Wow! Poor old Jennings!" Temple made a grimace of horrified excitement. Unfeelingly he said, "Good job they didn't take mine, too. Mine's still here, you see, propped up against . . ."

"All right, all right. You don't have to tell me fifty million times that your bike's still there. It's not *your* rotten old crock I'm worried about." Alarm and dismay seized Venables as he thought of the consequences of his high-handed action. "What's Jennings going to say when I go back and tell him that some thief has waltzed off with his super new bike! Why, I never even asked his permission to borrow it!"

It was indeed a distressing situation, and the unhappy culprit twisted his fingers in despair as he wondered how to cope with the unfortunate turn of events. It would have been bad enough if he had been using the bicycle with the owner's permission. But to have taken it without leave, and then to have allowed this to happen! How on earth could he face Jennings when he returned to school?

Temple was inclined to take a less gloomy view of the tragedy.

"Perhaps it hasn't been stolen after all," he suggested.

"Huh!" Venables rounded on him fiercely. "What else could have happened? You don't suppose it's free-wheeled itself back to school like a homing pigeon, do you?"

"No, but . . ." Temple scratched his nose thoughtfully. "Well, perhaps Jennings has taken it himself."

The brilliant deduction was dismissed with a snort of contempt. "You're crazy! How could Jennings have taken it when he's staying in all afternoon for Old Wilkie! Just tell me that, if you're so clever!"

This was unanswerable. Temple shrugged and said, "Maybe you're right. All the same, I shouldn't worry too much, until . . ."

"Oh, shut up! It's all very well for *you* not to worry. *I'm* the one who's going to get the blame. And don't just stand there like a spare dinner. Tell me what to *do*!"

Almost beside himself with worry, Venables' only thought was to hurry back to school at once and report the catastrophe to the sorrowing owner. Temple, on the other

126

hand, was in favour of making further investigations.

"Don't get in such a flap, Ven," he advised. "It won't help to rush off and tell Jennings – *he* won't know how to get it back. I reckon the proper thing to do is to inform the police."

"Yes, yes, of course – the police."

There was a telephone box farther down the road, and at Temple's suggestion they hurried towards it, intending to put through an emergency call without delay.

This, however, was not necessary. For as they approached the kiosk, Police Constable Honeyball, of the East Sussex Constabulary, chanced to cycle along the street on his tour of duty.

Venables was the first to see him. He rushed into the road waving his arms wildly and shouting to attract attention. "Hey! Stop! Police! Help! 999!" he called.

PC Honeyball dismounted and waited for the boys to catch up with him. "What's the trouble?" he demanded.

At once Venables broke into a flurry of explanation.

"Please, sir – I mean, please, Constable, there's been a robbery. My bicycle's been burgled while I was inside having fizzy drinks. Inside the café, I mean. And when I came out, there it was – gone!"

The policeman refused to be ruffled. "Let's get this straight, shall we?" he said. "Now, first of all, son, what's your name?"

"Graham Venables, of Linbury Court School."

The information was duly recorded in PC Honeyball's notebook.

"And you left your bicycle outside the café, and when you came out it had gone. Is that right?"

"Yes. Except that it wasn't really my bike. I borrowed it

from a bloke called Jennings," Venables explained. "Or rather, I didn't even borrow it. I took it without his permission."

"Be careful, Ven," Temple warned him. "You'll be arrested for pinching it yourself, if you don't watch out."

A look of alarm passed across Venables' worried features, and he did his best to make the facts clear beyond doubt.

"What I mean is, he didn't know I'd got it, but it would have been all right in any case, because he had to stay in and do extra history for Mr Wilkins."

By this time PC Honeyball's notebook was becoming filled with somewhat confusing data. *Borrowed without owner's consent, but all right because of history*, it said. Perhaps he would get on more quickly if he concentrated on a description of the missing machine, he decided.

This time there was no confusion. Both boys agreed that the bicycle was bright blue in colour, with white mudguards, a union jack on the lamp bracket and the owner's name on a label inside the saddle-bag.

"You can't mistake a bike like that," Venables added. "You can see it coming a mile off."

With this information at his disposal the constable felt that he had something definite to work upon. He promised to keep a look-out for a machine answering to this description, and to let the boys know the result of his inquiries.

"Thanks very much. That's really great of you, sir – I mean, Constable," said Venables. "And if you see anyone riding it, I should make a flying tackle and slip the handcuffs on him before he's had time to . . ."

He tailed off, aware from Mr Honeyball's expression that the policeman did not take kindly to hints on how to go about his business.

PC Honeyball stepped into the middle of the road.

"What I mean is – well, goodbye, and thanks for helping us," Venables amended.

After that, Temple mounted his machine and set off on the homeward trek. Beside him trotted Venables, wondering how best to break the tragic news when he arrived back at school.

PC Honeyball watched them go. When they were out of sight he glanced again at his notebook. *Bright blue bicycle... white mudguards... union jack on the lamp bracket...* You could see it coming a mile off, the boys had said.

At that moment the tinkle of a bicycle bell sounded close at hand. Looking up, the policeman saw two youthful cyclists riding down the street towards him. The foremost machine was bright blue in colour, with white mudguards. Furthermore, a small union jack was fluttering from the lamp bracket in front of the handle-bars.... There was no doubt whatever that this was the bicycle he was looking for.

With hand upraised, PC Honeyball stepped into the middle of the road to make inquiries.

Chapter 11

The Fateful Date

Jennings jammed on his brakes and brought his machine to a standstill in response to the constable's upraised hand. Why were they being stopped, he wondered? They were breaking no regulations that he was aware of. It was all very puzzling.

Darbishire, too, was completely taken aback by the unexpected command. "What's up, Jen?" he queried as he wobbled to a halt beside his friend. "We haven't been speeding in a built-up area, have we?"

Jennings shook his head. "Of course not. We've got nothing to worry about." He dismounted and turned to face PC Honeyball with a friendly smile – a smile which soon withered at the sight of the constable's forbidding expression.

"I want to have a look at this bicycle, son, if you don't mind."

Mystified, Jennings watched as the policeman took hold

of the handle-bars and ran his experienced eye over the machine. It took him only a few seconds to check the particulars with the description in his notebook. The facts were plain enough: the identity of the bicycle was established beyond question.

In official tones he said, "May I inquire where you got this machine from?"

Jennings stared at him in puzzled wonder. "Yes, of course. My Aunt Angela gave it to me for a Christmas present."

"Oh, did she!" PC Honeyball's voice was heavy with disbelief. "You did not, by any chance, find it outside Lumley's café further down the street?"

"Well, yes, as a matter of fact, I did," Jennings admitted.

"You're changing your story now. You just told me your aunt had given it to you."

"So she did, but that was about three weeks ago," Jennings explained.

"Three weeks! You want to be more careful what you say, son. Christmas was over and done with more than six months ago."

"Yes, I know, but she forgot, you see. I had to write and remind her because she's a bit absent-minded."

So far the boy's story did not sound very convincing. PC Honeyball looked at him sharply and said, "Let's get this straight. Did you, or did you not find this bicycle outside Lumley's café?"

"Well, if you mean this afternoon, yes, I did. I came along about twenty minutes ago and there it was, so naturally I took it."

"You took it," the policeman echoed in an ominous fashion. "You admit, in fact, that you stole this machine which you found parked outside . . ."

132

"Good heavens, no! I didn't *steal* it!" A look of horror and alarm spread across Jennings' features at the injustice of such an accusation. "Why on earth should you think I'd done that?"

PC Honeyball tapped his notebook with a large forefinger. "This bicycle answers to the description of a machine reported as having been stolen. I shall have to ask you to accompany me to the police station."

Panic and dismay seized the youthful cyclists, and Darbishire, who had been listening to the argument in open-mouthed wonder, blurted out, "You can't do that! It's really unfair accusing people of stealing their own belongings. Besides, who *said* it had been stolen, anyway?"

Consulting his notebook and speaking in slow, unruffled tones, PC Honeyball announced that according to information received from a certain G. Venables, of Linbury Court School . . .

He got no further, for at the mention of the informant's name Jennings almost choked with indignation.

"Venables! Coo, I could slaughter him!" he cried, incensed at the blackguardly behaviour of one whom he had thought to be his friend. "Just wait till I get hold of Venables! Just you wait, that's all! Riding off on my bike without permish, and then putting the police on my trail on a trumped-up charge!"

Darbishire was deeply shocked by the revelation. "Sabotage! Treachery! That's what it is!" he shrilled.

It took PC Honeyball a little while to stem the tide of righteous wrath which his news had evoked. At last, however, he managed to establish the fact that the outraged cyclist was claiming to be the owner of the "stolen" bicycle and therefore innocent of the charge levelled against him.

"I think I know what must have happened," Jennings went on when he had reached a calmer frame of mind. "You see, this bloke Venables thought I'd got to stay in this afternoon and do extra history."

The constable tipped back his helmet and scratched his head. This was the second time that the subject of history had been mentioned as having some bearing on the facts under discussion, but for the life of him he couldn't see just where it fitted in. By this time he had ceased to worry about the ownership of the bicycle. The fact that both sets of boys wore identical school caps suggested that the whole thing was no more than a misunderstanding. All the same, PC Honeyball was a painstaking officer who seldom abandoned a problem until all the facts had been brought into the light of day and scrutinised with care. His policy of never taking anything for granted had stood him in good stead in the past, when carrying out official duties.

"According to my information, the legal owner of this bicycle is a boy called Jennings – the same name that's inscribed in the saddle-bag," he said in a fresh attempt to straighten out the muddle.

Jennings nodded eagerly. "Yes, that's right. I'm Jennings and it's my bike."

"H'm! Anyone could *say* his name was Jennings. Can you prove it?"

It was Darbishire who hit upon the obvious solution. With a sweep of his hand he snatched his friend's cap off and thrust it under the policeman's nose. "There you are. Read the name on the name-tape," he cried. "That'll tell you who he is, right enough."

PC Honeyball recoiled slightly and focused his gaze upon the grimy lining of the cap. "C. E. J. Darbishire," he read aloud.

"Eh! Oh, fish-hooks! He must have come out in the wrong one by mistake. That's *my* cap he's wearing," Darbishire explained.

"This is getting worse and worse," complained Constable Honeyball. "Masquerading under the name of Jennings, while wearing a cap belonging to a person named Darbishire, and in possession of property reported stolen by an individual answering to the name of Venables." He shook his head doubtfully. "I don't get this at all."

"It's quite simple, really," Jennings hastened to explain. "You see, Darbishire's peg is next to mine, and we came out in a bit of a rush. I expect you'll find he's wearing my cap by mistake." Whereupon, he removed his companion's cap, hoping against hope that Darbishire was not inadvertently wearing headgear belonging to yet another person. It would confuse the issue still further if, for example, the name of Atkinson or Bromwich should appear on the tape.

Fortunately this was not the case. *J. C. T. Jennings* was inscribed in large letters on the lining, and with some reluctance PC Honeyball accepted this as proof of identity.

"It looks as though *one* of you must be Jennings, so I suppose it's all right," he said relinquishing the blue bicycle and retrieving his own machine parked against the kerb. "If I've got to start sorting out who is wearing whose cap, and who has got permission to ride whose bicycle – to say nothing of who is staying in to do whose history – we'll be at it till the cows come home."

In point of fact he was only too thankful of the chance

to wash his hands of this puerile problem, for he had more important duties to attend to. He was about to mount his machine when, on a sudden impulse, he turned and subjected Jennings to a long and careful stare. A flicker of recognition came into his eyes and he said, "Hey, wait a minute. I seem to remember I've met you before. Aren't you the lad who came to see me some time ago with a cock and bull story about a diary and secret codes?"*

Jennings gave a guilty start. Yes, of course! Now he remembered why the policeman's face seemed vaguely familiar. All the same, he was not anxious to discuss the matter, for it was one that had caused a certain amount of embarrassment to both parties.

He nodded in affirmation. "Yes, that's right. But I needn't really have bothered you, because I hadn't lost it after all, if you remember."

"Remember! Cor, stone the crows! I'm not likely to forget that caper in a hurry," PC Honeyball replied. "And seeing as you're the same lad, I'm not surprised you're in another spot of trouble now. Shouldn't think you're ever out of it for long, are you?"

The policeman's face creased in a wide grin as he swung his leg over the saddle and rode away down the street.

Jennings heaved a sigh of relief as he watched him go. The shock of being accused of stealing his own property, and the strain of proving his innocence, had left him feeling somewhat exhausted. Clearly, this was the moment to revive their flagging spirits with home-made cakes and bottles of fizzy drink, as he had suggested to Darbishire earlier in the afternoon. With this in mind they made their way along to Mrs Lumley's café and dismounted outside the garden gate.

*See *Jenning's Diary*.

"This is where my famous combination padlock's going to come in useful," Jennings observed. He placed the bicycles side by side against the garden fence and threaded through the front wheel of each machine the chain which he had just bought at the village stores.

"How's that, Darbi! If we chain the bikes together like this, nobody will be able to steal one without stealing both."

"But we don't want them to steal both," Darbishire objected.

"Don't be such a clodpoll. I didn't mean that," Jennings retorted. From his pocket he produced the padlock which sprang open at a touch, as the numbers had not been disturbed since his demonstration to Mr Carter in the staff-room. It was the work of a moment to slip the hasp through the links of the chain, and then came a loud click as the lock snapped shut. All that remained was to alter the numbers on the dial and the security arrangements would be complete.

"There you are. No one can possibly get that undone," Jennings said as he sent the rows of figures spinning round at random. "You couldn't open it, neither could Venables, nor even that suspicious policeman who thought he was so clever – unless, of course, he knew the combination."

"Well, for goodness' sake don't *you* forget it, or we shall be up a gum tree."

Jennings favoured his companion with a superior smile as he led the way in through the gate.

"Don't worry, Darbi. I couldn't possibly forget it. I told you, the numbers are the same as the date of the Spanish Armada."

"Oh, yes, of course," said Darbishire, relieved.

It seemed, on the face of it, a foolproof method of

remembering the combination. All that it entailed was the knowledge of a single historical date ... But, unfortunately, history was not Jenning's best subject.

Jennings was still nursing his feelings of grievance as he sat at the window table in Mrs Lumley's front parlour.

"I've met some snakes in the grass in my time, Darbi," he confided to his friend, when the proprietress had attended to his order for home-made cakes and fizzy drinks, "but I reckon Venables takes the bronze medal for treachery against allcomers. It was bad enough borrowing my bike without permish. But when it comes to calling in the police to organise manhunts for innocent victims – well, that's the last straw."

Darbishire nodded in solemn agreement. His voice came thick and muffled through an enormous mouthful of doughnut. "It's like those things that happen in *The Count of Monte Cristo*, or whatever the book is; where blokes get other blokes flung into dungeons on false charges, so the first lot of blokes can grab the other blokes' fortunes while they're languishing behind bars."

"Huh! If Venables thinks he's going to ride around on my bike while I'm languishing in some dungeon for pinching the thing, he's flipping well mistaken," Jennings said warmly.

After his third doughnut and his second glass of fizzy lemonade, however, his feelings of anger abated. A fourth doughnut restored his sense of well-being, and he was ready to forget his harrowing experience with PC Honeyball and turn his mind to other matters.

"Hurry up and swallow that last mouthful, Darbi, it's time we were going," he said, rising from the table and signalling to Mrs Lumley for the bill. "Mr Carter said we'd got to report to him by four o'clock – or else! He won't half create if we're not back on the dot."

The last drops of fizzy lemonade gurgled in Darbishire's drinking straw. Wiping his sticky fingers on the lapels of his jacket, he followed his friend out of the cottage and down to the garden gate, all set for the journey back to school.

Then the trouble started. Jennings bent down to open the padlock securing the two bicycles: a moment later he straightened up again, frowning with concentration.

"Just a sec. Let me think this out," he muttered. "It's the Spanish Armada, isn't it?"

"Yes, of course, and get a move on," Darbishire urged. "We've no time to hang about."

The frown of concentration deepened on Jennings' brow. "It can't be 1272 because that's Edward I, and I know it isn't 1805 because that's the Battle of Trafalgar."

A sudden suspicion that all was not well dawned in Darbishire's mind. "What on earth are you woffling about?" he demanded.

With an effort Jennings came out of his trance.

"Don't worry, Darbi," he said with an assurance he was far from feeling. "It's just that – well, I suppose *you* don't happen to remember the date of the Armada, do you?"

"Why, don't *you* know?"

"Yes, of course I do, but it's – sort of – slipped my memory for the moment," Jennings replied uneasily. "Don't panic, though. I'll remember it in time. That sort of thing often comes to you quite suddenly, when you're not thinking about it."

Darbishire was aghast at this revelation. He waved his

arms in the air and danced up and down in frustration.

"But, petrified paint-pots, what's the good of remembering it *later on*!" he cried. "We've got to know the combination right away, what with Mr Carter lying in wait for us and everything." He puffed out his cheeks in aggrieved protest and went on in scathing tones, "All that extra history you did for Old Wilkie in your own time! All that woffle about not possibly forgetting the date! All that . . ."

"All right, all right! Don't just stand there moaning like a foghorn," Jennings broke in. "Let's both try and think of the date."

It was all Venables' fault, really, Jennings explained. For had his feelings not been so outraged and his mind struck numb by the accusation of stealing his own bicycle, then he would certainly have remembered the fateful date. As it was, the strain of coping with police inquiries had reduced his brain to a honeycomb of bewilderment. How, in such circumstances, could anyone be expected to remember details of something that had happened in the Middle Ages!

For some minutes they racked their brains, trying to recall the one date in English History that would release them from their plight.

"Try 1381," Darbishire advised.

Jennings did so, but the padlock failed to respond. "That's not the Armada," he said, clicking his tongue in exasperation.

"No, I know it isn't. It's the Peasants' Revolt."

Jennings turned on his friend sharply. "You're crazy, Darbi! What's the point of telling me a date when you know all the time it's the wrong one!"

"Well, it comes out of the history book," Darbishire

defended himself. "And if your famous historical padlock was any good, it ought to know more than one date."

A quick glance at his watch caused Jennings to catch his breath in sudden alarm: unless they could start for home within the next five minutes they were certain to be late for the four o'clock roll-call. Desperate, now, they turned the digits of the padlock to every historical date they could call to mind . . . 1485 . . . 1605 . . . 1815. But all to no purpose. Clearly, none of these was the date of the Spanish Armada.

They were still twiddling two minutes later, when PC Honeyball cycled back through the village on his return journey.

"Still here?" he greeted them, halting by the kerb and regarding their antics with some amusement. "Haven't you sorted out whose bicycle is which yet?"

Darbishire flashed a nervous smile. "Oh, yes! But we've got into another muddle now."

"You don't say!"

"Yes, you see, we can't remember the date."

"That's easy enough," replied the policeman. "It's Saturday, July 10th."

"No, I don't mean *today's* date." Briefly Darbishire explained the dilemma of the chained bicycles, and the importance of arriving back in school in time to report to Mr Carter. "But unless we can remember when the Armada was, we haven't got a hope," he said bitterly. "I suppose you don't know any famous dates, do you?"

PC Honeyball scratched his nose in thought. It was thirty years since he had left school and the passage of time had dimmed his memory. "William the Conqueror, 1066," he hazarded.

Jennings sighed in despair. If that was the best suggestion the constable could offer, they would probably make
more progress without police assistance!

"I was never much good at history," PC Honeyball went
on apologetically. "Now if it was geography you wanted, I
could name all the capes and bays of the British Isles
for you. Let me see now: starting with the east coast of
Scotland, there's . . ."

"That won't help, I'm afraid. It's not a geographical
padlock," Jennings pointed out. "The trouble is we're
completely stuck without the combination. You see, we
can't even *push* the bikes with the wheels chained together
like this."

In spite of his shortcomings as a historian, it was PC
Honeyball who suggested the solution. The telephone
kiosk was only a few yards along the street. Surely the way
out of their difficulty was to ring up the school and ask one
of the masters to supply the information they sought.

"I suppose we'll have to," Jennings agreed doubtfully as
the police officer prepared to continue his journey. "But I
can just imagine what Old Wilkie will say if he answers the
phone. After all, this was one of the important dates I'm
supposed not to forget!"

Leaving their bicycles by the gate, the two boys hurried
to the call-box and squeezed inside. Jennings opened the
directory and thumbed his way through the pages until he
found the school's telephone number.

"Here we are: Linbury one-five-double-eight," he muttered, fumbling to place a coin in the coin-box.

Then he dialled the number.

It was Mr Carter's voice which sounded at the other
end of the line. "Hallo? Linbury one-five-double-eight,"
he said.

The words stirred an echo in Jennings' brain and for a few moments he remained silent trying to remember why they sounded familiar.

Puzzled by the silence, Mr Carter repeated his identity. "Hallo, hallo, who's there? This is Linbury one-five-double-eight speaking ... Linbury one-five-double-eight."

"Why, of course!"

With a cry of triumph Jennings slammed the receiver back on its rest, while Darbishire looked on in dumbfounded amazement.

"What on earth are you playing at, Jen?" he demanded. "What have you rung off for? You haven't even asked the question yet."

"I don't need to. Mr Carter's told me the answer," Jennings shouted in high glee.

"Eh?"

"Yes, he said, 'Linbury one-five-double-eight' ... Don't you see, Darbi, that's 1588 – the date of the Spanish Armada."

Flushed with excitement, he danced out of the callbox, warbling an improvised song in a high-pitched treble:

"Fifteen eighty-eight,
Now we shan't be late
Because we know the date
O tiddly-iddly-ate!"

By the time Darbishire rejoined his friend outside the café, the padlock was already open and the chain untwined. A few seconds later they were pedalling furiously along the road to Linbury Court. With luck they might still be back before Mr Carter had listed them as late-comers.

"You know, Darbi, these modern inventions are really useful for teaching you things," Jennings remarked as the school gates came in sight. "They didn't have telephone numbers and combination padlocks to help them remember their dates in the olden days – say round about 1588, for instance, did they?"

Darbishire thought this out as they pedalled up the drive and dismounted at the bicycle shed. "No, I suppose not," he said at length. "But on the other hand, if you'd lived all that long ago there wouldn't have *been* so much history, so you wouldn't have had so many dates to learn, would you?"

"That's a crazy argument," Jennings objected. "You might as well say that . . ."

But at that moment the school clock struck the hour. With one accord the two debaters abandoned their discussion and rushed headlong indoors to report their arrival to the master on duty, before it was too late.

Chapter 12

Alterations to the Programme

It was early the following week that Jennings conceived the idea of holding a Natural History exhibition. The thought came to him quite suddenly as he was cleaning his teeth one morning, and the more he pondered his plan the better he liked it.

The summer term still had another fortnight to run. Now was the time, he decided, to organise a public display of their zoological pursuits over the past eleven weeks. Accordingly, the secretary was instructed to notify all members that a meeting would be held in the tuck-box-room after prep on Wednesday evening.

"Now, all shut up and listen to my idea!" the Chief Frog Spotter began when the members had perched themselves precariously on the water-pipes. "The Head's been creating all through the term just because a few caterpillars got loose, and because one or two oiks happened to get a slight smear of mud on their shoes – and weedy, feeble excuses like that. Well, now's our chance to show him and everyone else that they've got the wrong idea about our club altogether."

"What do you suggest we do, then?" demanded Temple. "Clean our shoes, and show him a few caterpillars that *haven't* got away?"

"No, you clodpoll! What I mean is, we'll organise such a fantastic exhibition that he'll see we take the subject seriously. After all, it's just as good a hobby as stamps or history modelling, and he never moans about those."

"That's because he suggested them himself," Venables observed. "All the same, I don't see how you can have an exhibition unless you've got someone to come and see it, and who's going to do that?"

The Chief Frog Spotter flashed him a look of rebuke. It was some days since their quarrel over the borrowed bicycle – a quarrel which had ended in mutual handshakes after less then ten minutes' bickering. For all practical purposes they were again on friendly terms. Even so, Jennings decided, it would do the Chief Bird Watcher no harm to be taken down a peg or two.

"The trouble with you, Venables, is that you've got too much to say for yourself," he said with dignity. "If you'll only stop nattering for five seconds and listen to me, I'll tell you all about it."

Jennings' plan was simple. During the last week of term the annual presentation of prizes was held at Linbury Court. The ceremony was not regarded as a very formal occasion and, for this reason, parents living at a distance seldom attended the proceedings.

There were always, however, a few parents of day boys and local visitors who made a point of being present. Here, then, Jennings declared, was a ready-made audience who would be only too pleased to be shown round an interesting and well-planned exhibition.

"They always hang about for a bit after the prizes, in case there's a cup of tea going," he explained. "And that's the time to invite them in to see our stuff. We might even get the old character who doles out the prizes to come along, too, and that'd mean that the Head would have to come as well, and then he'd be able to see for himself that our club was a really good thing after all."

The proposal was hailed with enthusiasm by the members. A burst of applause broke out which lasted until Atkinson lost his balance on the radiator through clapping too vigorously, and crash-landed on to Rumbelow, squatting on a tuck-box below. This started an argument between the two of them which went on for so long that the original purpose of the meeting was lost, for the time being, in a welter of recriminations.

Darbishire was rather glad of the respite granted by the Atkinson-Rumbelow debate. As Honorary Secretary it was his duty to record the minutes of the meeting in his Nature Diary, and owing to the speed at which Jennings had outlined his plan, he was a few paragraphs behind the speaker. Now, however, he was able to catch up. Frowning thoughtfully, he rounded off his record of the proceedings up to date with the entry: *And having said all that the Ch. Fr. Spotter shut up talking (Cheers!)*.

At last the argument abated, and the meeting went on to discuss practical details.

What, Martin-Jones demanded, was the exhibition going to consist of?

"The same sort of things we've got already, only a lot

more – masses of them," Jennings decided. "And we'll put labels on the boxes to show what they are and what they eat, and write out a catalogue to give to everybody as they come in, and – and . . . Well, all that sort of thing," he finished up vaguely.

"That's all very well," objected Bromwich. "But there's over a week yet before the prize-giving, and Old Wilkie or someone is bound to kick up a hoo-hah if we go on filling up the common-room with *more and more* boxes of stuff."

Bromwich had certainly raised a point. The duty master was certain to register a protest if he found the common-room becoming more congested each time he visited it. He might – such was the limited understanding of grown-ups – ban their activities before they were complete, and thus give them no chance to show what a satisfying project the finished result was going to be.

"The less the masters know about it the better – until it's all ready, that is," Temple observed.

"Let's take our private possessions out of our lockers and put all the new specimens in them until the day before prize-giving. They'll be quite comfortable – there's plenty of air. And then, when we've got everything arranged and the masters see how fantastic it is, they're bound to let us go on with it."

The idea of *secretly* adding to their stock appealed to the members strongly. Surely, if the extra specimens were kept out of sight until the last moment, their plans would stand a better chance of succeeding.

"That's what we'll do, then," the Chief Frog Spotter summed up as the meeting closed. "Now, don't forget! Everyone is to collect as much stuff as possible by this time next week. If we all put our backs into it, we'll be able to put on a show that'll flipping well make people sit up and take notice."

In this, the Chief Frog Spotter was right. But just *how* right, he was unable to foresee at that early stage of the proceedings.

Jennings was not the only person to have given some thought to the programme for the following Friday week. Mr Pemberton-Oakes, also, held views on the subject of how a successful prize-giving ceremony should be conducted.

Some weeks previously he had written to invite the school's most distinguished Old Boy to attend as the guest of honour. Unfortunately, however, the plan had to be altered at short notice; and when Mr Carter paid a visit to the headmaster's study a week before the ceremony, he found his employer wearing a frown of disappointment.

"Ah, come in, Carter, come in," said Mr Pemberton-Oakes. "I'd like to have a word with you about the prize-giving. As you know, I was hoping that General Merridew would be able to come down and visit us again this year, but I've just had a letter to say that he hasn't been at all well lately – gout or something of the sort, I understand – and his doctor is strongly opposed to his carrying out an engagement of this sort."

"That's rather unfortunate," Mr Carter observed as he made himself comfortable in an armchair.

"It certainly is. I'm sure the boys will be most disappointed," the headmaster continued. "The general is such an old friend of the school, and I can always rely on him to say exactly the right thing on these occasions." He might have added that he could also rely on the general to say

149

exactly the *same* thing on these occasions, for every time he came down to his old school, General Merridew insisted on making a twenty-five-minute speech in which he repeated, almost word for word, the sentiments he had expressed on previous visits.

"It means, of course, that we shall have to invite someone else to give away the prizes," Mr Pemberton-Oakes said in tones of mild regret. "The trouble is that there's so little time left to make arrangements. In fact, between you and me, Carter, I am completely at a loss to think of any suitable person whom I could call upon at such short notice."

Mr Carter searched his mind and was obliged to confess that he, too, was unable to think of a substitute. Local celebrities, such as the Mayor of Dunhambury and the Archdeacon of the diocese, occurred to him as possible candidates, but in each case there was some perfectly valid reason why these dignitaries would be unable to attend.

"What we need," Mr Pemberton-Oakes emphasised, "is a man distinguished in the Arts, or education, a well-known explorer, an eminent scientist, or even, perhaps..."

"A scientist!" Mr Carter's face lit up in inspiration. "I have it! Why don't you ask Dr Hipkin?"

The headmaster looked puzzled. "Who?" he queried.

"Dr Hipkin. Don't you remember, HM? We met his wife during that cricket match at Bracebridge about a month ago. She told us then that her husband was well known in scientific and educational circles. He might be the very man we want."

Mr Pemberton-Oakes beamed with satisfaction. "An excellent suggestion, Carter. I'd forgotten about Dr

Hipkin. And now you come to mention it I remember reading somewhere – or did I hear it on the radio? – well, anyway, I have heard it from some source or other that he's regarded as a great authority in his particular line of research." With rising enthusiasm he went on, "I'll write to him at once. His address is sure to be in the phone book."

As Mr Carter was about to take his leave, the headmaster was struck by a further thought.

"There's just one thing, Carter," he said, leaning back in his chair and studying the lampshade with great intensity. "As a classical scholar I must admit to a certain ignorance in scientific matters. Do you, by any chance, happen to know in which particular branch of science Dr Hipkin specialises?"

But this time Mr Carter was unable to help. "Sorry, HM. I've no idea," he was obliged to confess.

The prospect of having to present the prizes at Linbury Court School threw Dr Hipkin into a flurry of nervous terror when he read the headmaster's letter at breakfast the following morning. He gave a start of agitation, choked over a mouthful of toast, and nearly spilt his coffee down his waistcoat. "Oh, my goodness! How perfectly dreadful!" he mumbled in stricken tones.

Mrs Hipkin stared at her husband in surprise. "Whatever's the matter, Basil?" she demanded.

The doctor put down his coffee cup with an unsteady hand. "I've had a letter from a man named – er – um – Pemberton-Oakes, I think it is, asking me to give away the prizes at a school called Linbury Court next Friday."

"Splendid!" approved Mrs Hipkin.

"It's very kind of him, of course, and I'm deeply

151

honoured, but . . ." Dr Hipkin paused, and a slight tremor shook his slender frame. "Unfortunately, he wants me to make a speech as well, so I'm afraid it's quite out of the question."

"Nonsense!" boomed Mrs Hipkin in a voice that set the milk jug rattling in echo. "Of *course* you'll accept the invitation. A man of your knowledge and reputation is just the right sort of person to deliver an inspiring message to the youth of today."

Her husband groaned inwardly. "I don't mind handing out the prizes," he said. "It's what comes afterwards that worries me. The thought of standing up on a platform and making a speech to all those rows of shiny pink faces is too frightening to contemplate!"

Dr Hipkin's dilemma arose from the fact that he was, by nature, of a shy and retiring disposition. Addressing an audience was, for him, an ordeal from which he shrank in alarm. Even on scientific subjects in which he was an expert, he seldom spoke in public, unless badgered to do so by his wife.

"I don't know why you're making such a fuss," Mrs Hipkin said in disparaging tones. "There's nothing to be nervous about in talking to a lot of little boys. They won't eat you."

"No, perhaps not, but . . ." The doctor racked his brain to think of a watertight excuse. "Well, you know I'm never at ease with strangers. I've not met this man Pemberton-Oakes before, and . . ."

"Don't let that worry you. I've met him, and he's perfectly charming," his wife replied promptly. "He's the headmaster I spoke to on the day those two boys pulled you out of the river."

"Really? How very interesting. Yes, I remember those boys well," Dr Hipkin murmured. "So they are pupils at Linbury Court, are they?"

"Oh, no. They go to Bracebridge School – a different place altogether," Mrs Hipkin replied. To the best of her knowledge this statement was correct, and it was certainly not her fault that the information was somewhat wide of the mark. "Anyway, Basil, if you're worried about making a speech, I'll compose one for you," she offered.

"You will!" There was a note of relief in Dr Hipkin's voice and he flashed a smile of gratitude across the breakfast table. For what *really* caused him such concern on these occasions was not so much the presence of an audience as the fact that he could never think of anything to say.

But if his wife was willing to help . . . If he could conceal her carefully written address behind a stack of prize books or a vase of flowers, then, surely, his troubles would be over . . . At any rate, he would not have to worry about his mind becoming a complete blank when the moment arrived for him to make his speech!

"Well, that's very kind of you, my dear," the doctor said in tones of quiet satisfaction. "And if you *really* insist on my going through with this nerve-racking ordeal . . ."

"I certainly do, Basil."

". . . then in that case I'll drop a line to Mr Pemberton-Oakes and say I shall be very honoured to accept his invitation."

The members of the Natural History Club were not idle during the week that followed. Inspired by the enthusiasm of the Chief Frog Spotter, they collected a shoal of tad-

153

poles, and a large selection of crawling creatures which they secreted in jamjars and matchboxes in their lockers in the common-room.

Thursday was D-Day, and six o'clock was zero hour for the exhibits to be taken from their hiding-places and arranged for public view. By 6.30 the common-room was teeming with various forms of insect life. Caterpillars crept, newts nibbled and beetles burrowed in an endless row of cardboard boxes stretching along the window-sill and overflowing on to the floor. Foliage for fodder was piled high on the table, and all about the room lay a trail of twigs and dead leaves, dropped by the naturalists on their journeys to and from the lockers.

Mr Wilkins was the master on duty on the day preceding the prize-giving. Bustling with efficiency, he strode round the building when tea was over, making sure that all the rooms were looking smart and tidy in readiness for the great event. When he reached the common-room, however, a shock awaited him.

"Good heavens! What on earth's going on in here!" he gasped as his eye took in the rows of cardboard boxes and the trail of decaying vegetable matter. Curtly he turned upon the curators of the small-scale menagerie. "Come along now, you boys. Clear away all this clutter at once, and let's have this room properly tidied up."

Cries of protest and dismay went up on all sides of the room.

"Oh, but, sir! It's our exhibition, sir!"

"Specially in honour of prize-giving, sir."

"Yes, sir, and we've been to an awful lot of trouble, sir."

"We were planning it as a special secret surprise, sir."

Mr Wilkins had scant sympathy for the plans of the

entomologists. "I dare say, but I'm not having any capers of this sort, today of all days, thank you very much," he told them. "There's a very important visitor coming to present the prizes tomorrow, and the Head wants the place looking its best. All those boxes will have to be put out of sight in the cupboard, and the rest of the rubbish thrown in the dustbin."

"Oh, but, *sir*!"

"Be quiet, Jennings. You heard what I said. Do as you're told, at once!"

The exhibitors pulled long faces, shook their heads and clicked their teeth in disappointment as they set about the task of tidying up.

"It's always the same," Atkinson grumbled beneath his breath. "Whenever we organise anything fabulous we're never allowed to go on with it." Somewhat sulkily he added, "What's the name of this man who's coming tomorrow, sir?"

Mr Wilkins frowned in thought. He had gleaned from the headmaster a few details about the distinguished guest, but for the moment the name had slipped his memory.

"Dr Somebody-or-other. Hopkins or Hipwell or some name like that," the master replied. "Anyway, he's a famous scientist."

The news did something to dispel the atmosphere of gloom and frustration.

"A scientist! Wow!" Venables exclaimed. "I'm reading a book about a scientist who invents a new sort of atomic rocket. He goes zooming about in a plastic suit with zip fasteners and things." With rising curiosity he asked, "Do you think this man who's coming tomorrow will be wearing a space-suit, sir?"

"Don't talk such ridiculous nonsense," retorted Mr Wilkins. "I don't imagine Dr What's-his-name is that sort of scientist at all."

"*Is* there another sort then, sir?" Venables demanded in surprise.

Mr Wilkins tut-tutted with impatience. "Whatever sort of scientist he is, he won't want to wade ankle deep through dead leaves and boxes of caterpillars, so stop talking nonsense and get this room cleared up quickly."

"Yes, sir." Obediently, Venables knelt down and began mopping a trail of pondwater on the floor-boards with a makeshift duster.

"No, no, no, boy! *Not* with your handkerchief!" the duty master exclaimed in exasperation. At that moment his eye lighted upon the tadpole aquarium, in which a score of specimens in the later stages of development were darting about amongst the pond-weed.

"And I'm not having that tank of repulsive reptiles on the window-sill! Put it somewhere out of sight, Jennings," Mr Wilkins ordered.

The Chief Frog Spotter made a gesture of despair. "But there's nowhere else to put it, sir," he complained. "It's too big to go in the lockers, and anyway they're full of caterpillar boxes already, sir."

A quick glance round the room confirmed the truth of this remark. Perhaps, after all, it would be better to leave the aquarium in its customary place.

"All right then," Mr Wilkins conceded grudgingly. "But don't blame me if the headmaster raises objections when he sees it. He's coming round tomorrow morning to make sure the building is looking shipshape for the ceremony."

"Oh, I'm sure *he* won't mind, sir," Jennings replied. "After all, a few harmless tadpoles couldn't possibly be a nuisance to anyone, could they, sir?"

Mr Wilkins made no reply as he moved away to supervise the removal of beetle boxes and caterpillar cages from the other end of the room. It was, perhaps, as well for his peace of mind that he could not foresee the trouble that a few harmless tadpoles were to cause him during the course of the following day.

Chapter 13

Disappearing Trick

The boys were all in class when the headmaster, accompanied by Mr Carter, made his tour of inspection on Friday morning.

"Dr Hipkin will be arriving shortly after lunch, so we must have the school looking its best," he remarked to his assistant as they ascended the stairs. "Between you and me, I'm going to have a word with him in private before the ceremony. I'm most anxious to find out some more details about his scientific career, so that I can mention it in my – ah – little speech of introduction."

"You haven't had time to find out very much about him, I take it?"

"Unfortunately not. His letter accepting my invitation made no mention of his work, so I've not yet been able to discover whether his speciality is chemistry, or biology – or even atomic physics."

"Let's hope it's not that," Mr Carter said with a smile.

"I don't think our prize-giving ceremony would be quite a suitable occasion for splitting atoms."

"Quite! We will hope for nothing more alarming than a split infinitive, eh, what?" Now in an excellent humour, the headmaster purred with laughter at his little joke as he led the way into the common-room. At first glance everything seemed neat and tidy, and he was about to leave the room when he noticed an object that caused the smile to fade on his lips.

"What on earth are those squirming objects in that bowl on the window-ledge?" he demanded.

Mr Carter inspected the contents. "Tadpoles, without a doubt. Big ones, too: they'll be turning into frogs any day now," he reported.

The headmaster drew in his breath sharply. "I hardly think that the common-room is *quite* the right place for – ah – amphibia of this kind," he observed. "Normally, I am only too keen to encourage an interest in natural history, but as we want everything in apple pie order for Dr Hipkin's visit, I think it would be better if this – ah – collection was removed for the time being."

"Very well, HM. I'll get Robinson to take them away as soon as I go downstairs."

Robinson, the caretaker, obeyed his order to the letter when he entered the common-room ten minutes later. His instructions were to remove the tadpoles: Mr Carter had said nothing about the tank in which they were kept. To some extent this was an unfortunate omission, for the caretaker was a methodical worker who took a pride in doing exactly as he was told – no less and no more.

Accordingly, he fished about in the water with an

improvised net until all the specimens had been caught and carefully deposited in the bucket of water which he had brought with him for this purpose. Then he trudged across to the pond, and returned the tadpoles to their natural surroundings.

Shortly afterwards the bell rang for the end of morning school. Jennings had to stay behind after Form Three were dismissed, for he had orders from Mr Wilkins to tidy his desk. He was halfway through this tedious task, when the door flew open and Darbishire, wide-eyed with woe, burst into the room.

"I say, Jen, something terrible's happened!" he gasped out. "Have you been into the common-room lately?"

"No, not since last night. Why?"

"Well, I've just come from there, and there's been a ghastly catastrophe . . . *The tadpoles have all escaped!*"

Jennings stared at his friend in blank amazement. "What on earth are you talking about?" he demanded.

"The tadpoles! I tell you they've escaped. Gone, vanished, disappeared!"

"But that's crazy! They *can't have.*"

"I tell you they *have!*" Darbishire cried wildly, waving his arms and marking time as though taking part in some primitive war dance. "Don't just stand there saying they *can't* have, because I can prove it. Come and see for yourself, if you don't believe me."

In breathless haste the two boys raced off to the common-room and skidded to a halt by the window-sill, where, for some moments, they stood gaping at the aquarium in puzzled wonder.

The pondweed was still floating on the surface. The stone grotto still rose up from the gravel on the floor of the tank. The water level was unchanged: only the wriggling occupants were missing.

"I was right, you see," Darbishire said with gloomy satisfaction. "And it's no good you staring at it with your eyes popping out like organ stops. The whole perishing lot of them have got loose, and that's that."

"But I don't see how they could have done it," Jennings persisted. "They were all there when we went to bed last night, and they couldn't get out, unless – unless . . ."

The words tailed off as a possible explanation occurred to him . . . The whole batch had been in an advanced stage of development: for the past week their tails had been shrinking, and the first signs of limbs had been growing more noticeable every day. It was, indeed, for this reason that Jennings had built the pyramid of stones reaching above the surface of the water, so that any newly graduated frog could stretch its legs and enjoy a breath of fresh air in comfort.

Could this be the answer to the mystery? Was it reasonable to assume that the whole batch had grown their legs during the course of a single night, and had organised a mass-escape? . . . At first sight it seemed difficult to believe. But what else could account for the empty tank?

"I've got it, Darbi – *legs*, that's the answer," Jennings announced dramatically. "They must have found their feet while we were in bed, and then climbed up on to this stone diving-board and hopped over the side."

"Wow! Fully fledged frogs!" Darbishire was appalled at the thought. "What a gruesome bish! There'll be a frantic hoo-hah if Sir gets to hear about it. Supposing he finds a whole plague of them croaking and playing leap-frog round the library, or somewhere. It's enough to make your mind boggle."

"I know. Mine's boggling on both cylinders," Jennings agreed. "Come on! We'd better start rounding them up before anyone finds out they're loose."

A quick glance round the room was enough to show that there was no sign of their quarry. Obviously, Jennings reasoned, the frogs had travelled far and wide, and the only hope of retrieving them lay in a systematic search of landings and adjoining rooms. Unfortunately, their plans to begin the hunt forthwith were thwarted by the sounding of the lunch bell, and they were obliged to postpone operations until after the meal was over.

"We'd better keep quiet about it till we've had a chance to round them up," Jennings advised as they went into the dining hall. "The fewer people who know about this, the better."

"Yes, of course," Darbishire agreed. But the thought of the possible consequences filled him with apprehension and took the edge off his appetite. "This is frantic," he bemoaned, while waiting for his portion of curried rice to be passed down the table. "All the time we're sitting here eating, those frogs will be hopping farther and farther away."

"Can't be helped," Jennings muttered. "Anyway, we've got at least an hour before the prize-giving. That should give us enough time to find them."

Immediately after the meal, the two boys scampered upstairs to begin the search. First, they scoured the common-room from end to end, ransacking the cupboards and lockers and poking behind the bookcase. Then, they moved next door to Form Five B classroom, hoping to

meet with more success, but they had not been searching
long before a loud voice and heavy footsteps were heard
approaching along the corridor ... A moment later the
door was flung wide, and Mr Wilkins marched across the
threshold.

"Now what are you boys doing in here?" he demanded,
as his glance fell upon Darbishire rummaging through the
waste-paper basket, and Jennings, perched on a desk,
examining the top of a bookcase.

Darbishire rose from his knees. Hesitantly he said, "I
was just looking for – er – for some things, sir."

"Oh, were you! Well, this is no time to start spreading
the contents of the waste-paper basket all over the floor,"
Mr Wilkins reproved. "And what are you doing up there,
Jennings? Admiring the lamp-shade?"

"No, sir. I was just trying to find – er – what Darbishire's trying to find," Jennings explained. "I was searching high, while he searches low, sir."

It was clear from his expression that Mr Wilkins was not satisfied with this vague explanation. It was also clear that the flight of the frogs could not be kept a secret indefinitely, for at any moment a chance croak might reveal their whereabouts. All things considered, it might be better, Jennings thought, to confess what had happened before it was too late to put matters right. Surely Mr Wilkins would be bound to agree that the whole thing was an accident due to circumstances beyond human control!

"It's like this, sir," Jennings began. "You remember those tadpoles you saw in the common-room yesterday?"

"I certainly do."

Jennings gulped and swallowed hard. "Well, sir, I'm afraid there's been an unfortunate accident. They're not there any more... They've sort of – removed themselves."

Mr Wilkins eyebrows shot up in surprise. "Talk sense, boy. Tadpoles can't walk."

"They can when they're frogs, sir," Darbishire explained sadly. "At least, they can hop. You see, they all hatched out during the night when we weren't there, and then they must have climbed up on to a stone that we'd put sticking out of the water, and got out over the side of . . ."

But Mr Wilkins didn't wait to hear the end of the sentence. With a strangled cry he dashed from the classroom to investigate the truth of this alarming theory. Half a minute later he was back, fuming with exasperation.

"You silly little boys!" he stormed. "You've let the whole lot of them escape! I might have known this would happen."

"Sorry, sir," said Jennings humbly.

"Sorry! So I should think. We've got to get them back immediately. Where have the wretched things hopped off to?"

"That's the trouble, sir. We don't know," Jennings replied. "You see, they've had quite a good start, and they might be anywhere by now. All in different places, I shouldn't wonder."

A sound like the application of a vacuum brake forced its way through Mr Wilkins' vocal cords.

"I – I – *Corwumph!*" he spluttered. "This is intolerable. Frogs at large all over the building, with an important visitor due to arrive at any moment! What's he going to think if he's greeted by swarms of repulsive reptiles leaping out from every doorway, and croaking at him at the tops of their voices!"

The Chief Frog Spotter and the Honorary Secretary fidgeted with embarrassment, and stared down at the toes of their shoes, while Mr Wilkins strove to bring his outraged feelings under control.

There was only one thing to be done, the master declared, when he had reached a calmer frame of mind. A thorough inspection of the premises must be organised, and the fleeing amphibia collected without delay. Why, there must be twenty or thirty of the wretched things hopping about, judging from the number of tadpoles he had seen in the tank the previous evening.

"Every available boy must start looking at once," he ordered. "We must comb the building from end to end, and find every one of these frogs before the guests arrive."

But, unfortunately, it was already too late to carry out this plan exactly as Mr Wilkins intended. For even as he finished speaking, Venables and Atkinson appeared at the open door of the classroom.

"Oh, there you are, sir. We've been looking everywhere for you," Venables announced.

"What is it?" Mr Wilkins snapped irritably.

"Please, sir, we just saw an estate car drive up on the playground, and an old man get out, sir."

The news affected Mr Wilkins strangely. He clapped both his hands to his head and tottered round in small circles. "Oh, my goodness gracious! Here, already!" he moaned when he had ceased revolving.

"He didn't look much like a famous scientist to me," Venables complained. "He wasn't wearing a space-helmet – just a floppy old hat as ancient as a school bun. I was hoping he'd have one of those plastic suits with zip fasteners and . . ."

"Be quiet, Venables!" Mr Wilkins broke in. "We haven't a moment to lose." Rounding on Jennings and Darbishire, he barked out, "Go on, you boys. Go and start looking at once. Try the library, to begin with."

"Yes, sir." Obediently they hurried from the room, while Venables and Atkinson stared after them with rising curiosity.

"And you two, as well. Go and find some more boys and start searching," Mr Wilkins commanded.

Atkinson looked blank. "But what are we supposed to be searching *for*, sir?"

"Tadpoles – I mean, frogs. I want you to find as many as you can."

"Why, sir?"

"Never mind why. Do as you're told." This was hardly the moment, Mr Wilkins felt, to embark upon a long-winded explanation; though, in point of fact, it would have prevented a great deal of misunderstanding later on if only he had made plain the reason for his unusual instructions.

"And you'd better tell anyone else you see to do the same," he ordered as he strode towards the door. "There should be twenty or thirty of them about, so mind you look properly."

Atkinson continued to look puzzled. "Well, supposing we *do* find some, what shall we do with them, sir?"

"Report to me at once. I want to make sure we've got the lot."

In the doorway Mr Wilkins caught sight of two more third-formers approaching along the corridor. Brusquely he called, "You two boys, there! Come here, you're wanted."

Temple and Bromwich trotted up expectantly. "Yes, sir? What is it, sir?"

"Urgent job for you. Venables will explain what you have to do."

So saying, Mr Wilkins hurried along the corridor and swept down the stairs two at a time. It was essential that he, himself, should be on hand to welcome the guest of honour at the front door. For if this duty were left to anyone who was not aware of the present crisis, the doctor would be shown into a room which, not having been searched, might well be infested by the plague of hopping amphibia.

The thought of the eminent scientist imprisoned in the library amongst a swarm of frogs leaping from chair to chair caused Mr Wilkins to take the last three stairs at one bound and shoot across the hall like a sprinter breasting the finishing tape. Panting slightly, he opened the front door and beamed a welcoming smile at the small figure in the grey suit and well-worn hat, who was standing on the top step waiting for his ring to be answered.

"Good afternoon, Dr – ah – um – Dr Hipkin," Mr Wilkins said, remembering the name at the last moment with a great effort of memory. "Do come in. My name's Wilkins. If you'll come with me, I'll take you along to the Head's study."

Dr Hipkin forced a wan smile and made a nervous, throat-clearing sound by way of reply.

"It was very good of you to come at such short notice," the duty master went on in chatty tones. "I know all the boys are looking forward enormously to hearing your speech."

"My speech," Dr Hipkin echoed faintly. "Oh, yes, yes, of course."

His hand fluttered towards the inside pocket of his jacket as though seeking comfort from the crinkle of the vital manuscript. The next moment an expression of alarm transfigured the doctor's mild features. He pulled the pocket inside out and stared horror stricken at two bus tickets and an assortment of grey fluff which was all that the lining contained.

Feverishly, he began feeling through all his other pockets while Mr Wilkins regarded him curiously, and gathered up the handkerchiefs, fountain pens, pencils and spectacle case which, in his nervous flurry, the doctor kept dropping all over the doorstep.

"Oh, my goodness! This is terrible!" he muttered when a thorough search of all his pockets had failed to produce the sheet of paper which he needed so desperately.

"Can I do anything?" Mr Wilkins asked.

"No, I'm afraid you can't. Something most unfortunate has happened. A disaster – a catastrophe!" Dr Hipkin blurted out in tones of agitation.

"Oh, but surely! If you'll come along with me to find the headmaster, perhaps he could . . ."

"Good gracious, no! I can't do that! Not yet, anyway. I must have time to think this out. I'll be back later."

Whereupon, Dr Hipkin turned and hurried down the front steps and round the corner, leaving Mr Wilkins staring after him in a state of puzzled indecision.

Clearly the guest was somewhat ill at ease and would need sympathetic handling, Mr Wilkins thought. But this was really nothing to worry about. Obviously he had left something (the notes for his speech, perhaps?) in his car, and would be feeling far more confident and assured when he returned in a few moments' time.

The moments ticked by, but Dr Hipkin did not appear. The moments became minutes and still there was no sound of footsteps crunching on the gravel to announce the guest's return.

Worried, now, Mr Wilkins hurried down the steps to see what was wrong. As he turned the corner, he could see the estate car parked on the playground, but there was no sign of the driver.

Mr Wilkins strained his eyes in all directions. The playground was deserted! An exasperated "Corwumph!" broke from his lips as he set off round the angle of the building to look for the missing guest.

This really was the limit, he told himself, frowning with annoyance . . . Disappearing frogs were bad enough, but disappearing guests – well, that was the last straw!

Chapter 14

The Scientific Frogman

Venables shook his head in a pitying manner as Temple and Bromwich came hurrying into Form Five B classroom in accordance with the duty master's instructions. "I reckon Old Wilkie's gone clean round the bend this time," he said.

"Why, what's up?" Temple inquired with interest. "He said you'd tell us what the excitement was all about."

"It's about frogs," Atkinson chimed in. "He wants us to collect as many as we can."

The newcomers exchanged glances. "Are you pulling our legs, Atki?" Bromwich demanded.

"No, honestly. He told Venables and me to start searching at once. We've got to round up all we can find, and the more the merrier."

"But what does he want them *for*?"

Atkinson shrugged. "I don't know. Perhaps he's thinking of joining our Natural History Club. The point is, where can we get some?"

A triumphant smile spread over Venables' features. "I've just thought! I know where we can find hundreds," he announced proudly.

"Goodo! Where?"

"In the bushes behind the cricket pavilion. I saw a whole lot there about a week ago, while I was looking for a lost ball. Big ones, too!"

"Fair enough! Let's go and start hunting," Atkinson suggested. "Just you and me, eh, Venables?"

"What about us?" Temple queried. "We've got to find some as well, don't forget."

Bromwich tapped him on the shoulder. "You come with me, Temple. I happen to know there's any amount of them in that ditch behind the 2nd XI cricket nets."

"Come on, then! What are we waiting for?" Temple exclaimed, hurrying towards the door. "If it's frogs Old Wilkie wants, we'll find him so many he won't know what to do with them all."

In the circumstances there was some excuse for this unfortunate interpretation of Mr Wilkins' wishes. Apart from the Chief Frog Spotter and the Honorary Secretary, none of the boys had been into the common-room since the headmaster's inspection, so they had no means of filling in the gaps in the duty master's surprising instructions.

While this discussion was taking place in Form Five B classroom, Jennings and Darbishire were engaged in a thorough search of the library. Naturally enough, their quest was in vain, and when at last it became obvious that no slippery fugitives were lurking in the darker recesses of the room, Jennings felt convinced that their quarry must have fled farther afield.

"I reckon we're barking up the wrong tree, Darbi," he said, poking underneath the radiator with a broken ruler. "They may not be indoors at all. Put yourself in their place: if you were an escaping frog, where would you go?"

"As far away from Old Wilkie as I could get," Darbishire replied with feeling.

"There you are, then! I bet you they've all beetled back to the pond. They've probably got a strong homing instinct."

"What – like pigeons?"

"Well, *something* like. Anyway, if we go down there and have a look, I dare say we'll find them sitting around in the reeds croaking with laughter at us."

Darbishire straightened up from his inspection of the lower shelves of a bookcase. "Maybe you're right," he agreed.

Accordingly, they abandoned their search in the building and hurried out of doors to the pond at the far end of the playing-fields. On the way they discussed the problem of what they should do if their quest was successful.

"There's no point in carting them all back indoors if we find them," Jennings decided. "Old Wilkie will only tell us to chuck them in the pond again."

"Yes, I know, but we've got to try and account for them all before we report to him," Darbishire argued. "And what's worrying me is, how are we going to tell *our* frogs from any others that happen to be hopping about?"

"Oh, that's easy. Our lot will be tiddly little things. They only moved up from being tadpoles a few hours ago."

They were passing the cricket pavilion at that moment and, as they drew level with the entrance, Venables and

Atkinson trotted down the steps carrying an old cricket bag between them.

"We're going to use this to put the frogs in when we've caught them," Atkinson explained. "Venables says he knows where there are masses, so we'll need something pretty roomy."

A sudden suspicion crossed Jennings' mind. "Yes, but look here, it's no good just catching *any* old frogs. Sir only wants *special* ones."

"That's all right. They'll be *extra* special by the time we've finished choosing them. We'll only pick out the best specimens," Venables sang out over his shoulder, as he and Atkinson disappeared round the corner of the pavilion.

Jennings felt vaguely troubled. It seemed to him that Venables and Atkinson had completely misunderstood the whole point of Mr Wilkins' instructions. However, they would find out their mistake in due course, and in any case, he and Darbishire couldn't stop to argue while so much remained to be done.

"I'm pretty sure Venables has got things round his neck, as usual," Jennings remarked as they resumed their journey. "He's making a big mistake if he thinks he's going to please Old Wilkie by taking him a lot of frogs he doesn't want."

"You can't please Old Wilkie, whatever you do," replied Darbishire. "In fact, the more you go out of your way to be nice to him, the less he seems to like it. He's like one of those blokes in a story my father once told me about . . ."

"Look, Darbi!" Jennings' urgent tone cut across his friend's flow of prattle and brought him to a sudden halt.

"Why? What's up?"

By way of reply Jennings pointed to a clump of trees edging the pond some fifty yards distant. Pacing up and down in a distracted manner was an elderly gentleman in a grey flannel suit and an ancient trilby hat. At that distance they could not recognise his features, though there was something about them that struck Jennings as being vaguely familiar.

Puzzled and curious, they made a stealthy approach, though in point of fact their caution was wasted on the elderly man, who was so wrapped up in his thoughts that he would not have noticed an approaching herd of buffalo.

A few yards farther on Jennings stopped again, and his eyes lit up in recognition. "Why! I know who it is!" he exclaimed, seizing his friend by the elbow.

"Eh! Who?" Darbishire peered short-sightedly through his dusty lenses, his expression blank with ignorance.

"It's Dr Hipkin. The old character in the panama hat that we pulled out of the river. Don't you remember?"

"Yes, of course I remember. But this bloke isn't wearing a panama hat. He's wearing a trilby."

Jennings flipped his fingers in exasperation. "Don't be such a dehydrated clodpoll, Darbi! Surely he can have two hats if he wants to. Besides . . ." He broke off as the obvious explanation of Dr Hipkin's presence flashed into his mind. "Yes, that's right! His wife told us he was a scientist, didn't she?"

"Maybe she did, but I should want proof before I believed a thing like that," Darbishire objected. "After all, look at his moth-eaten old hat. It's not what you'd call a *scientific*-looking hat, is it? And that old panama he was wearing on the river wasn't much better, either."

"Oh, for goodness' sake! Can't you leave his hats alone and focus your shrimp-witted brain on what he's doing here!" Jennings cried impatiently. "Don't you see! Dr Hipkin must be the distinguished scientist who's going to give away the prizes this afternoon."

"Wow, yes, of course!" Darbishire exclaimed in sudden understanding. Indeed, now he came to think of it, the facts fitted perfectly. They had been told to expect a scientist; according to Venables the visitor had arrived in an estate car. That, surely, was conclusive proof that their old friend, Dr Hipkin, was to be the honoured guest of the afternoon.

"But what's he doing mooching about down here by himself?" Darbishire queried. "He ought to be in the Head's study getting ready to dole out the prizes."

Jennings shrugged. "Perhaps he's got lost. Come on! Let's go and ask if we can help."

He led the way forward at a lively trot and accosted the visitor in welcoming tones. "Good afternoon, Dr Hipkin. Do you remember us – Jennings and Darbishire?"

The doctor came out of his trance with an effort of will.

"Eh? What's that?" he murmured in a far-away voice. Then he gazed long and earnestly at the two figures smiling up at him, and gradually memory stirred and he beamed back their smiles of welcome.

"Why, yes, of course! You are the boys who came to my rescue when my skiff capsized," he said in delighted recognition. "But what are you doing here? I understood from my wife that you went to school at a place called – er – um . . ."

"Bracebridge?" prompted Jennings.

"Yes, that's right. Fancy meeting you at Linbury!"

Jennings and Darbishire averted their gaze and shifted uncomfortably.

"Well, it's like this. We do *really* go to school here. We

made a bit of a bish when we explained things to Mrs Hipkin," Darbishire confessed. "You see, what happened was . . ." He would have gone on to explain in more detail, had not his friend butted in and changed the topic of conversation.

"We saw you wandering about and we thought perhaps you'd got lost, sir," Jennings said hastily. "Would you like us to show you the way to the Head's study?"

A look of alarm spread over Dr Hipkin's thin features. "Good gracious, no. Heaven forbid! I'm not nearly ready to meet him yet. In fact, between you and me, I've come down here by myself specially to get *away* from the headmaster."

They stared at him in surprise. This, surely, was an odd way for a guest to behave!

"But aren't you going to come and make a speech at the prize-giving?" Jennings demanded.

Dr Hipkin clasped his hands and looked uncomfortable. "I shall never bring myself to do it," he twittered. "All those boys sitting there staring at me – anxious to hear some stirring message. The prospect is quite unnerving."

Jennings could hardly believe his ears. "But you couldn't possibly be frightened of *us*, sir," he said in blank astonishment. "We're ever so well behaved – during prize-giving, I mean. We shan't throw tomatoes or walk out in the middle, or anything like that."

"No, we couldn't, even if we wanted to," Darbishire added reassuringly. "You see, we have to sit through it to the end, however boring it is."

Dr Hipkin shook his head. "You don't understand. It's not your behaviour I'm worried about. It's having to stand up and make a speech, when I cannot for the life of me think of anything to say."

Briefly, the doctor recounted his problem. He told them how his wife had insisted on his accepting Mr Pemberton-Oakes' invitation, and had overcome his fears of addressing an audience by writing out in full the speech he was to deliver. This practical help had eased his mind considerably, he explained, and he had set out for Linbury Court with every confidence – only to discover upon arrival at the front door that he had left his precious manuscript behind.

"And now I can't remember a single word of the speech," he lamented. "It's more than fifty years since I attended a function of this sort, and I've no idea what is the right thing to say on these occasions."

It was Jennings who suggested the remedy.

"That's all right, sir. We know the drill," he volunteered. "We've listened to old – er – to distinguished visitors doling out the prizes so often that we almost know it by heart, don't we, Darbi?"

His friend nodded in agreement. "That's right. They all say the same things, you see, year after year – especially General Merridew."

The shadow of despair faded from Dr Hipkin's eyes and he stood looking at his young friends with the eager expression of a spaniel hoping for a biscuit.

"In that case I should be most grateful for any help you can give me," he assured them, fumbling in his pocket for an odd scrap of paper on which to jot down the words of wisdom as they fell from Jennings' lips.

"Well, sir, you start off by saying, 'My first duty is to congratulate the prize-winners upon their splendid achievements,' " Jennings began. He paused for thought and then went on, "And after that, you cheer up the blokes who've come bottom of the form by telling them that they're just as clever as the others, really. What you should say is: 'I never won a prize when I was at school and look at me now.' "

Dr Hipkin looked vaguely troubled. "But I *did* win prizes when I was at school. I seem to remember that I was considered particularly bright."

"In that case I should try and play it down a bit," Jennings advised. "General Merridew always laughs his head off when he tells us what a duffer he was when he was our age."

"That bit usually starts off, 'The race is not always to the swift,' " Darbishire put in. "And then you say, 'School-days are the happiest time of your life.' " He uttered a mirthless laugh. "I know it sounds crazy, especially if you're in Mr Wilkins' form, but it's all part of the treatment."

"Really! Most interesting!" murmured Dr Hipkin, scribbling rapid notes on the back of an envelope. "This is extremely valuable information. Now tell me, what else does one say?"

"Well, after that you tell us to put our shoulders to the wheel and keep a straight bat."

"Not both at the same time, surely," Dr Hipkin protested. It sounded to him a somewhat uncomfortable contortion.

"Well, you know what I mean," said Jennings. "Oh, yes, and then you go on . . ."

In five minutes they had provided him with a summary of all they could remember having heard from previous speech day visitors. It was probably the only case on record of an orator's address being composed by members of his audience.

"Of course, there's a lot more you *could* say, but it's better not to," Jennings finished up. "General Merridew usually comes out with a whole lot of gobbledygook about Education coming from the Latin word *educare*, but if you take my advice you'll skip that bit. You see, the shorter the speech the louder we'll clap."

"Splendid," smiled Dr Hipkin.

"Oh, yes, and there's just one more thing. Whatever you do, you *must* ask for a half holiday before you sit down."

Dr Hipkin beamed his thanks. He felt quite confident now about the task awaiting him . . . *Congratulate prize-winners warmly* . . . *Lukewarm congrats to non prize-winners* . . . *Race not always to swift* . . . *Happiest days of life* . . . *Straight bat* . . . *Shoulder to wheel* . . . *Half holiday.* With this vital formula on the back of his envelope he felt he could not go wrong.

"We'll have to be going now, sir," Jennings told him. "You see, we've got to catch some frogs rather urgently for one of our masters."

A flicker of interest showed in Dr Hipkin's eyes. "Frogs! But how splendid! I'm delighted to hear that your masters encourage you to take an interest in natural history."

"Well, it's not quite so simple as that, sir," said Darbishire, remembering Mr Wilkins' panic-stricken orders.

"Perhaps you would allow me to help," Dr Hipkin went on. "In fact, I should be most grateful if you would let me repay your valuable assistance by showing you a simple trap – an invention of my own, I might say – constructed from a few twigs, which I find very useful for the purpose of collecting frogs and other amphibia in large numbers."

They stared at him thunderstruck. "But you can't come round catching frogs with *us*," Jennings protested. "I mean – after all, you're a famous scientist."

Dr Hipkin blinked modestly. "I should hesitate to call myself famous," he said diffidently. "But as a zoologist I suppose I may claim a certain reputation in scientific circles."

"Zoologist!" Jennings gasped in surprise. "You mean you're only a frog scientist after all!"

"Oh, yes. My interest is purely in amphibia such as the common frog, the indigenous toad, *rana temporaria* . . ."

Jennings and Darbishire exchanged glances. Somehow, they felt vaguely cheated. Surely a scientist should be an exciting, mysterious figure, an expert on satellites and space-ships . . . And here was Dr Hipkin admitting that he was nothing more than a scientific frogman. It was all rather disappointing! However, they could hardly refuse to co-operate when the guest of honour was anxious to go to such trouble on their behalf.

Obediently they followed as Dr Hipkin picked his way through the bulrushes to a spot on the far side of the pond which his experienced eye told him would be a suitable place to demonstrate his frog trap.

Chapter 15

Present for Mr Wilkins

The prize-giving ceremony was due to begin at three o'clock. At twenty minutes to the hour, when the local guests were beginning to arrive, a wild-eyed, flustered Mr Wilkins burst into the masters' common-room bearing tidings of woe.

"I say, Carter, this is fantastic," he blurted out to his colleague, who was getting ready to attend the function. "Dr Hipkin has vanished."

Mr Carter frowned. "Surely not. His car has been outside on the playground since just after lunch."

"Maybe it has, but the distinguished guest isn't *inside* – or anywhere else on the premises, so far as I can make out."

At first sight, *The Mystery of the Disappearing Scientist* contained all the baffling ingredients of a detective story. Dr Hipkin had been seen to arrive. Reliable witnesses had watched him alight from his car and make his way round the corner of the building. Mr Wilkins, himself, had spoken to him at the front door. But from that moment onwards his movements were unknown, and a search of the building from cellar to attic had failed to provide any clue to his whereabouts . . . And with the prize-giving ceremony due to start in twenty minutes' time, it was small wonder that Mr Pemberton-Oakes was treading his study like a cat on a hot tin roof demanding to know what had become of his guest.

"I tell you I'm fed up with the whole business," Mr Wilkins complained when he had finished recounting the facts. "I've had just about enough of chasing round the school after disappearing scientists – to say nothing of sending boys chasing round after disappearing frogs."

Mr Carter raised a puzzled eyebrow. "Disappearing frogs? I'm afraid I don't follow."

A shadow of anguish passed across Mr Wilkins' face as he recalled the horrifying situation he had been obliged to cope with directly after lunch.

"Believe it or not, Carter, that silly little boy, Jennings, had a collection of overgrown tadpoles in the common-room yesterday afternoon."

"Yes, I know. I saw them."

"Well, what you *don't* know is that the miserable reptiles hatched out into frogs during the night, and escaped all over the school. I've got Venables and Temple and several other boys looking for them at this very moment."

A suspicion flashed into Mr Carter's mind that his colleague was barking up the wrong tree. "What makes you so sure they've escaped?" he asked.

"I've got eyes," Mr Wilkins retorted. "I saw them in the tank yesterday, and when I went in there after lunch today they'd all gone."

Mr Carter tut-tutted gently. "Oh, yes, they'd gone all right, but not of their own accord," he explained. "The Head thought they were unsightly, and on his orders I told Robinson to remove them before Dr Hipkin and the rest of the guests arrived."

"What!" The room swam before Mr Wilkins' eyes. He rocked on his heels and leaned heavily against the bookcase for support. "What! You mean to say . . .! And there was I organising frog-hunting parties left, right and centre. Dash it all, Carter, you might have told me!" Muttering darkly, he sank into an armchair and ran his fingers distractedly through his hair.

Mr Carter refused to regard the matter as a major tragedy. "Don't look so hot and bothered about it, Wilkins," he advised. "Surely you can stop worrying, now you know that there aren't really any frogs at large in the school after all."

He spoke too soon. For at that moment a knock sounded on the staff-room door, and Temple and Bromwich marched into the room carrying a large cardboard box with holes pierced in the lid.

"Please, sir, we've brought you some frogs," Temple announced proudly.

"F-f-frogs!" Mr Wilkins shot from his chair like a rocket from its launching base.

"Yes, sir. A whole boxful. Do we get a reward, sir?" Bromwich chimed in. "We found them in the ditch behind the cricket nets, sir."

Mr Wilkins appeared to be in the grip of some powerful

emotion. "*Doh!* Take them away at once, you silly little boy," he moaned. "I didn't say I wanted *any* frogs. I said you were to catch the ones that had got loose in the building."

Temple looked puzzled. "Which ones would those be sir?" he queried.

"I – I . . . There weren't any, as it happened."

The look of bewilderment deepened in Temple's eyes. "But if there weren't any, sir, why did you ask us to catch them?"

"Oh, go away, both of you, and take those repulsive reptiles with you!" Mr Wilkins cried in exasperation.

Disappointed, the boys withdrew, but no sooner had their footsteps died away along the corridor, than another knock sounded on the staff-room door.

"Come in," called Mr Carter.

This time the visitors were Venables and Atkinson. From the throbbing movements going on inside the cricket bag they carried, it was clear that their hunt behind the pavilion had yielded good results.

"Please, sir, we've brought some frogs for Mr Wilkins," Atkinson said, beaming from ear to ear with a sense of duty nobly done.

A squawk of protest broke from the lips of the outraged duty master. Incapable of speech he flung his arms upwards and marked time upon the hearth-rug, and it was left to Mr Carter to explain that the gift was unacceptable.

"But Mr Wilkins *told* us, sir," Venables protested. "He said . . ."

"Maybe he did," Mr Carter broke in. "But that doesn't alter the fact that he no longer wishes you, or anyone else, to bring any more frogs to the staff-room."

"Please, sir, we've brought some frogs."

"Yes, sir," Venables heaved a sigh of frustration. Why couldn't masters say what they meant, like ordinary civilised human beings! A little sulkily he asked, "Well, what shall I do with them, sir?"

"Let them go again, of course."

"Yes, sir." Venables stooped to pick up the cricket bag, and Mr Wilkins, mistaking his intentions, was galvanised into a shout of protest.

"No, no, no! Not in *here*, you silly little boy. Take them back where you found them."

As they were about to leave, Atkinson was struck by a sudden thought.

"Had we better go and tell the rest of the blokes to stop collecting, sir?" he asked. "Practically everyone in Form Three is going round the cricket field trying to find some for you, sir. Take Jennings, for instance: I happen to know he's . . ."

"Oh, my goodness!" A fresh tremor of indignation passed through Mr Wilkins' powerful frame. "If any more boys come knocking at the door bringing me unsolicited parcels of hopping amphibia, I'll – I'll . . . Well, they'd better *not* come knocking at the . . ."

His words died away as another tap sounded on the staff-room door. Livid with anger, he crossed the room in three strides determined to put an end, once and for all, to these infuriating visitations.

"Now look here," he shouted, hurling the door open with all his strength. "I've had just about enough . . ."

The stream of protest ceased abruptly. For the latest visitor was no inky-fingered third-former clutching a box of hopping amphibia. It was M. W. B. Pemberton-Oakes Esq, MA, Headmaster.

There was a moment of pained silence. Then, as the headmaster's eyebrows slowly sank to their normal level, Mr Wilkins stammered, "I'm terribly sorry, HM. I beg your pardon. I didn't know it was you. I was – er – I was expecting some frogs."

The eyebrows rose again. "Frogs, Wilkins?"

"Well, you see, I've just been brought two batches and I thought you were the third frog-former – I mean third-former – that is . . ."

Interesting though the subject was, this was hardly the moment, Mr Pemberton-Oakes felt, to listen to a rambling account of the hobbies and habits of Form Three.

To begin with, the bell for the prize-giving ceremony was due to sound in less than ten minutes' time, and so far he had not yet set eyes upon the guest of honour, nor discovered in which branch of science he was regarded as an authority. With mounting impatience the headmaster said, "Really, Wilkins, I cannot waste another moment discussing frog-formers – er – third-formers and their frogs. Will you kindly tell me at once where Dr Hipkin is?"

Mr Wilkins spread out his hands in a helpless gesture. "I'm sorry, HM. I haven't been able to find him."

"But this is ridiculous. Do you realise . . .?"

"Oh, sir, please, sir," Venables interrupted urgently.

"Be quiet, boy!" snapped the headmaster.

"But, sir, I know where he is, sir! *I've seen him.*"

The three members of the staff wheeled round in unison.

"Where?" they chorused.

"Down by the pond, sir. We saw him talking to Jennings and Darbishire as we came round by the pavilion, didn't we, Atkinson?"

His friend nodded in agreement. "That's right, sir. They went down there to try and find some frogs for Mr Wilkins' collection."

"*Doh!*" A low moan whistled through the lips of the master on duty. He smote his brow with a tragic gesture and went for a short walk round the table to relieve his feelings.

"But if you don't want them after all, it doesn't really matter, sir," Atkinson went on when the master had tottered to a standstill. "I mean, they won't be wasted, because they'll come in useful for our Natural History Club."

Mr Pemberton-Oakes drew in his breath sharply. He was not in possession of the full facts of the matter, yet it seemed to him that it was largely due to the misguided efforts of the naturalists in Form Three that the prize-giving ceremony was in danger of becoming a complete fiasco. Sternly he addressed the Keeper of Moles and Voles (if any).

"Judging from what I have heard, Atkinson, this Natural History Club of yours has already caused a considerable amount of chaos and confusion. That being so, I have no intention whatever of allowing it to be carried on any longer." With a frown of impatience he turned to his two assistants. "Carter, will you go along to assembly hall at once and see that the boys are all in their places ready for the prize-giving?"

"Certainly, HM."

"You come with me, Wilkins," the headmaster went on. "We must hurry down to the pond and find Dr Hipkin without a moment's delay."

It was not often that Mr Pemberton-Oakes moved about

the school grounds at anything faster than a dignified walk. And, therefore, it came as something of a shock to the boys streaming into the assembly hall for the prize-giving ceremony, to see their headmaster, accompanied by Mr Wilkins, hurrying across the playing-fields at a lively canter. Clearly, something sensational was afoot!

At the edge of the pond the two masters panted to a halt, and stared with unbelieving eyes at a trio of figures just visible among the reeds on the far side.

"Good heavens! Bless my soul! Words fail me!" gasped Mr Pemberton-Oakes . . . For there, ankle-deep in mud, crouched the guest of honour beaming with delight at a large bull-frog squatting in the palm of his hand. Flanking the guest on either side were the mud bespattered figures of Jennings and Darbishire, listening with keen attention to a short lecture on the feeding habits of the common frog.

When he had recovered his breath, and his power of speech, the headmaster led the way round to the far side of the pond. In spite of his inward turmoil, his manner was suave and charming as he extended his hand to greet the elusive visitor.

"Ah! How do you do, Dr Hipkin. I'm so glad you were able to come," he said with a watchful eye on the bull-frog now hopping about at his feet.

The doctor's features creased in a nervous smile as he rose to his full height. Furtively he wiped his muddy hand on his trouser-leg before returning his host's greeting. "How do you do, Headmaster. I do hope I'm not late. These boys have been showing me . . ."

"Quite, quite," the headmaster interposed, freezing Jennings and Darbishire with an icy glare of disapproval. "Though for the life of me I cannot imagine what on earth

189

possessed them to detain you in such – ah – unsuitable surroundings. However, I shall deal with them in due course – and with appropriate severity." Whereupon he raised his right eyebrow a couple of centimetres as a signal to the boys to withdraw from the scene without further delay.

Dr Hipkin was quite taken aback by their sudden, ignominious departure. "Oh, please don't punish them," he protested in dismay. "They have been most helpful to me – most helpful indeed. Besides, it was all my own fault, I assure you. It was I who suggested that this side of the pond would be a suitable place for catching frogs in large numbers."

The headmaster blinked and looked helplessly at his colleague.

"I understood from my young friends here," Dr Hipkin prattled on mildly, "I understood that one of your assistant masters is keenly interested in forming a collection of amphibia . . ."

A choking sound, not unlike the cry of a bull-frog, rattled its way through Mr Wilkins' vocal chords. Then he coughed and blew his nose loudly to conceal his embarrassment.

". . . and, of course, being a zoologist myself, I can't tell you how delighted I am that Natural History is so keenly studied in your school."

"Natural History!" echoed the headmaster faintly. "Oh – ah – yes, of course!" Now, for the first time, Mr Pemberton-Oakes became aware of the subject in which Dr Hipkin was so eminent an authority.

"The boys have been telling me about their collections of tadpoles and caterpillars," the doctor continued. "I need hardly say how much I am looking forward to inspecting them and, perhaps, proffering a word of advice and encouragement."

The headmaster pursed his lips and frowned thoughtfully. It was less than five minutes since he had informed Atkinson in no uncertain terms that the Form Three Natural History Club was an enterprise which would no longer be tolerated in any circumstances . . . And yet, with so eminent a zoologist as Dr Hipkin pleading its cause, what could he do? There was nothing for it but to agree to the doctor's request.

"Yes, yes, of course. I'm sure the boys will be delighted to show you their collections," the headmaster replied with as much enthusiasm as he could muster. Then, turning to his assistant he added in an undertone, "Perhaps you will arrange for the – ah – the specimens to be displayed in the common-room after prize-giving."

Mr Wilkins blenched visibly. It was only the previous afternoon that he had gone to all the trouble of having them removed. However . . . "Very well, HM," he said with an effort.

"And now, Doctor," Mr Pemberton-Oakes went on with a furtive glance at his guest's soaking shoes and mud-plastered hands. "I really think it is time we went indoors to prepare for our little ceremony. The procedure is quite informal. I shall, naturally, call upon you to say a few words after you have presented the prizes."

"Oh, my goodness!" For a moment Dr Hipkin was seized with a sudden panic.

Then he remembered! From his pocket he produced a crumpled envelope and studied it intently for some seconds. He felt better then: and as he followed his host back across the playing-fields and into the school buildings his lips moved in silent rehearsal.

"Congratulate prize-winners ... Congratulate *non*-prize-winners ... Race not always to the swift ... Happiest days of your life ... Straight bat ... Play the game ... Shoulder to the wheel ... Half holiday."

Thanks to Jennings and Darbishire, Basil Featherstone-haugh Hipkin, Esq, DSc, FZS, looked forward with quiet confidence to the duty that awaited him in the assembly hall.

Chapter 16

The Trouble with Grown-ups

In spite of the turmoil and confusion which marred the early part of the afternoon, the annual prize-giving ceremony started only twenty minutes later than its advertised time.

The ceremony itself was uneventful and largely followed the pattern of previous years. Mr Pemberton-Oakes made a speech in which he dwelt at some length upon the school's health, sporting record and academic achievements, and skimmed rather more hurriedly over various other activities (the Natural History Club, for example), which had not been an unqualified success.

In the front row sat the prize-winners with hair neatly parted, finger-nails spotless, and knees and faces polished and gleaming. One by one they marched self-consciously up on to the platform in shoes which seemed to have developed a piercing squeak specially for the occasion.

Blotwell, R. G. (prize-winner in Form One) bowed so

193

low in receiving his award that he nearly bumped his head on the table. Bromwich (top of Form Three and honourable mention in Mathematics, Art, Geography, French and Latin) was so encumbered with his prizes that he had difficulty in shaking hands with the guest of honour: while Pettigrew, winner of the Fourth Form prize for general progress, was so taken aback by the applause which greeted his appearance, that he dropped the book he had just been given and, stumbling to pick it up, kicked it off the platform into the audience.

Jennings and Darbishire sat in the back row and clapped each prizewinner until their palms were tingling. They themselves had won no prizes, but – who could tell? – perhaps their turn would come next year . . . *Perhaps!*

Then came Dr Hipkin's address. When once he had actually started to speak, his nervousness disappeared, and he found to his surprise that the ordeal was not nearly so frightening as he had expected.

The information kindly supplied by Jennings and Darbishire stood him in good stead. With an occasional glance at the envelope concealed behind his programme, he was able to deliver an abbreviated version of the same speech that the boys had heard from General Merridew the year before. The only difference was that, as Dr Hipkin's speech was shorter, it was applauded more loudly.

His concluding sentence, in which he asked for a half holiday, was felt by the younger members of the audience to be such a soul-stirring appeal that it would have melted the heart of even the sternest headmaster . . . And Mr Pemberton-Oakes, who had guessed what was coming, granted the request – as he always did, year after year.

When the ceremony was over, the guests were hustled

away to the headmaster's study for tea, while Mr Wilkins made hasty arrangements to have the Natural History Exhibition displayed in the common-room for their inspection.

"Come along, you boys, look lively now," he boomed as he strode into the room, where a crowd of boys were admiring the prize-winners' books. "Open the cupboard and get out all those boxes of wriggling caterpillars and horrible earwigs and things. Line them all up along the window-sill, and put the overflow in tidy rows on the floor."

The ex-members of the banned club stared at him in surprise. What on earth was the man talking about?

"But, sir, you told us to pack them all away out of sight yesterday," protested Bromwich. "You said Dr Hipkin wouldn't want to see them lying about."

"Maybe I did. And now I'm telling you to get them all out again. The headmaster wants the Natural History Club to arrange a display as quickly as possible."

The stares of surprise grew into looks of blank uncomprehending bewilderment. Clearly, the man was as mad as a hatter!

"But, sir, that *can't* be right," Atkinson insisted. "The Head told me himself after lunch that he wasn't going to allow the Club to go on any more, sir."

"He's changed his mind," Mr Wilkins replied shortly.

"Has he, sir? You mean – like you did over those frogs you told us you wanted, and then decided you didn't?"

"Yes – er – no! Oh, don't ask silly questions!" snapped the duty master. "Start getting those caterpillars lined up for inspection."

Encouraged by this welcome, though baffling, reprieve,

the third-formers set about their task with a will. Flinging wide the locker doors, they brought forth their boxes teeming with insect life and arranged them in a tasteful display. Once more caterpillars were crawling, beetles burrowing and newts nesting from end to end of the common-room. Leaves lay strewn about the floor, and twigs crackled underfoot as the impromptu exhibition took shape.

Jennings watched his fellow naturalists at work with mixed feelings. He was glad that the exhibition was going to be held after all, for it was he who had suggested the idea in the first place ... And yet, his aquarium which should by rights have been the centre of attraction, was devoid of the tadpoles which he had amassed with such loving care. It seemed unfair that he alone of all the Club members had nothing to show for the work he had done.

Even Darbishire had his Nature Diary, he reflected, as he caught sight of his friend arranging the precious book on the table, in such a way that it was bound to catch the eye of the spectators.

"Hey, Darbi, mind you leave the diary open at that page where you wrote down a record of my tadpoles," Jennings ordered. "It's the only proof I've got that I ever caught any at all."

Darbishire looked uncomfortable. "Sorry, I can't, Jen. I had to tear it out."

"What!" The Chief Frog Spotter was incensed at this act of vandalism. "What did you want to do that for?"

"I didn't *want* to, but it had a big blot on it. I had a slight accident with a leaky fountain pen."

"Well, I like the cheek of that! How's anybody going to know ..."

"What I thought would look rather splendid," Darbishire interposed hurriedly, "would be to have the book lying open at the first page -- where I wrote that nature poem about the feathered songster and drew butterflies and things around the edges."

Jennings snorted in disgust. "Huh! Feathered songster! Why couldn't you have done one about my tadpoles instead?"

"You can't have feathered tadpoles," the poet objected.

"Maybe not. But at least you could have drawn some, instead of a lot of weedy butterflies. You never thought of that, I suppose."

"Well, no, I didn't actually," Darbishire admitted. "But there's still room in the margin if you want to have a bash." So saying, he moved away to help Martin-Jones to recapture a lively cockroach which had escaped from its box.

Left to himself, Jennings ran his eye over the opening page of the Nature Diary. Yes, there *was* room for a few tadpoles, he decided, and anyway, it was only right and proper that there should be some tribute to their remembrance.

Frowning with concentration, he drew a series of blobs with tails of varying sizes all down the right-hand margin. Then he focused his attention on Darbishire's poetic masterpiece, proudly displayed in the middle of the page.

Hark how the feathered songster sings,
As it soars aloft on fluttering wings.
If thou, O bird, couldst also speak,
What words would warble from thy beak?

At this point the fountain of poetic inspiration had dried

up, leaving a space of four lines underneath ... Just enough room for an epitaph to the tadpoles, Jennings decided. He chewed his pencil for some moments while his muse was being invoked. Then he wrote:

Of tadpoles, we did have a tankful,
For which we were most humbly thankful.
But as it happened they got away
Which is why they are not on show today.

It may not have been deathless verse, but on the whole it wasn't at all bad, Jennings decided as he read the lines over to himself. Even the severest critic would agree that his poem was every bit as good as Darbishire's feeble effort about songsters nattering through their beaks.

While the exhibits were still being arranged and the hubbub was at its height, the door opened and the head-master ushered Dr Hipkin and a bevy of other guests into the room.

Just for one moment Mr Pemberton-Oakes felt a pang of dismay at the disorderly sight that met his gaze. On all previous occasions he had taken pride in ensuring that the school was looking its best when the speech-day visitors were shown round. Now, his tidy mind was shocked to see the common-room looking like a jumble sale struck by lightning.

He need not have worried! For nothing could have given the guest of honour greater pleasure than the sight of so much zoological zeal.

"Oh, but how splendid!" purred Dr Hipkin. "This takes me right back to my schooldays. I always say one is never too young to start taking an interest in entomology."

198

"Quite! Most instructive and – ah – educational," the headmaster agreed. Honesty compelled him to add, "Though, frankly, Dr Hipkin, I must confess that the Natural History Club has been something of a problem in the past. So much keenness tends to disturb the smooth running of school routine, you understand."

"Oh, but I'm quite sure you won't curb their enthusiasm," reproved the doctor, to whom the smooth running of school routine meant less than nothing. "That would be a disaster – a catastrophe."

Mr Pemberton-Oakes stroked his chin thoughtfully. Perhaps the doctor was right. Perhaps it would be better to give the Club his official blessing. After all, he prided himself on being progressive!

He waved his hand in a tolerant fashion at the bustle and commotion going on all around them. "You needn't worry about that, Doctor," he said. "Just look at them. You can see for yourself how anxious I am that the boys shall enjoy their hobby to the full."

"Splendid, splendid," murmured Dr Hipkin, as he started off on his tour of inspection. In painstaking detail he examined the small-scale menagerie, pausing at each cardboard box to offer advice and information about its wriggling inmates. Behind him hovered the headmaster and Mr Wilkins, whose encouraging smiles seemed to suggest that Natural History was a subject which had always been accorded pride of place at Linbury Court School.

At the common-room table the doctor spent some while straining his eyes over the pages of the Nature Diary, while the delighted author stood first on one foot and then on the other, twisting his fingers and curling his toes in a positive agony of self-conscious pride.

A few minutes later Dr Hipkin drew to a halt beside the aquarium and peered down into the water as though certain that there *must* be some creature lurking in its depths if only he could see it. Perhaps there was something hiding beneath the stone grotto, he thought, and pushed his spectacles up on to his forehead, in the hope of locating the object of his search.

"There *should* be some tadpoles, but they've all gone, sir," Jennings said apologetically. "They hatched out while we weren't looking, and got away."

"That's just where you're wrong, Jennings," Mr Wilkins broke in unexpectedly, and then went on, in genial tones, to explain the misunderstanding.

It came as a surprise to the Chief Frog Spotter to hear the details of the alleged escape. But what surprised him even more was the manner in which Mr Wilkins told the story.

". . . so you see, it was really too funny for words! There was I imagining the worst, when, in point of fact, the situation was completely under control," Mr Wilkins finished up with a bellow of laughter that set the windows rattling.

Jennings stared at him in dumbfounded amazement. Why should Mr Wilkins now treat the whole thing as a joke? Only two hours earlier he had been storming with indignation at what he then seemed to regard as one of the major disasters of the· twentieth century. It was all very well to be tactful in the presence of guests, but this sudden change of attitude was most bewildering . . . But then, masters always *were* unreliable in matters of that sort!

"What d'you think of that, Darbi?" Jennings whispered to his friend as the official party moved on to inspect Temple's puss-moths. "I reckon Old Wilkie's got a sauce.

He comes stonking round after lunch moaning like a brace of fog-horns about our tadpoles and now look at him – grinning like a slice of melon and saying how funny it was!"

Just for a moment a flicker of resentment showed in his eyes. "Besides, the whole thing's a mouldy chizz," he grumbled. "All the other oiks had got masses of caterpillars and things to show Dr Hipkin, and I'd got nothing but an empty tank."

Darbishire nodded sympathetically. "Never mind, you can soon fill it up again. After all, the Head's bound to let the Club go on now the exhibition's been such a success. He wouldn't have the nerve to put a stop to it with Dr Hipkin backing us up like this."

"Yes, I know." The shadow of disappointment faded and the wide-awake look came back into Jennings' eyes. "Still, it proves what I've always said about grown-ups – they don't see things in the same way as sensible people like you and me . . . And all that stuff they woffle about when they stand up and make speeches just doesn't make sense at all."

Darbishire looked puzzled. "How do you mean?" he queried.

"Well, look what happens! When *we* want to keep tadpoles and things, the Archbeako starts creating. You'd think they were man-eating crocodiles to hear him talk. But as soon as some old character comes along who left school about a hundred years ago, the Head says what a good idea it is . . . And then they get up and make speeches about this being the happiest time of your life!"

Jennings heaved a sigh of long-suffering resignation as

he watched the headmaster's party wend its way across the room. He shook his head sadly. "You never know where you are with grown-ups, do you!"